Beyond the Setting Sun

RASPBERRY RIDGE
BOOK SIX

JESSIE GUSSMAN

Contents

Acknowledgments

Cover art by Julia Gussman
Editing by Heather Hayden
Narration by Jay Dyess
Author Services by CE Author Assistant

Listen to the unabridged audio for FREE performed by Jay Dyess on the Say with Jay channel on YouTube. Get early access to all of Jay's recordings and listen to Jessie's books before they're available to the general public, plus get daily Bible readings by Jay and bonus scenes by becoming a Say with Jay channel member.

W esley Moffat, hockey superstar and potential author, if his agent had anything to do with it, sat on the front porch of the lake house he'd bought not long ago. Staring at the water, and contemplating his future.

His agent had insisted that if he had any hope of repairing his reputation in the professional hockey league, he would need to get his autobiography finished by the time his suspension was over and he was allowed to join his teammates on the Virginia Icebreakers.

He couldn't imagine a life without hockey, although he'd come close to losing everything. He needed to get this book done.

The publishing world worked slower than a tortoise, and the book wouldn't come out until next summer, but hopefully by then, he would have helped his team win the championship cup, and the book would just be the icing on top. If anything else went wrong, it might help fans understand why he was the way he was, according to his agent, and perhaps save his reputation and career.

Wesley didn't give a flip about his reputation, but his career was important to him.

And he was back to where he started. He couldn't imagine his life without hockey.

He sat and stared at the computer in front of him. Lots of folks he knew had ghostwriters, and Wesley could get on board with it. The only problem with a ghostwriter was details of his memoir might be leaked, and that would ruin everything according to his agent, Jim.

Jim was good at what he did, but sometimes he could be a little bit paranoid, at least in Wesley's opinion.

"It's a little burnt, but it's edible." His grandfather lived with him so when Wesley went to the beach for the summer, he came with, came out of the screen door of the cabin—no air conditioning—and handed him a plate of...maybe chicken?

Neither one of them could cook worth anything, and they were close to being in danger of starving. There were no fast-food restaurants in Raspberry Ridge.

He'd picked the town out, not because of its beautiful views of the lake, but because of its seclusion and isolation. There shouldn't be any paparazzi or anyone who would actually recognize him. Especially if he kept a low profile.

The downside was, when one of them burnt supper, there were no fast-food restaurants within thirty minutes.

Tonight, it was Gramps's turn to burn supper. Last night, it had been him. Fish. Fish wasn't his favorite anyway, and it almost tasted better burnt. Gramps didn't think so, but people could have other opinions from him. They could be wrong.

"Thanks. This is a little better than the fish last night," he said agreeably.

"The fish was terrible. At least this is only burnt on one side."

He took the fork that Gramps handed him and lifted up the meat to see that indeed the side that was down on his plate was only partially burned.

"You're definitely getting better. I think you probably ought to be the full-time chef."

Gramps snorted. "If your grandmother could hear you now," he started.

"She'd agree with me wholeheartedly. She always said you needed to learn."

Gramps snorted again, but he knew he was right. Grandma passed away three months ago, and neither one of them had gotten over her passing yet. In fact, that might have had something to do with the fact that he had gotten suspended for the first month of the season.

He might have been a little sensitive about it at the time, flying off the handle when he shouldn't have.

Unfortunately, he already had the reputation of a hothead, and what he had done had turned out worse than what he had intended.

No one was hurt any more than needing a few stitches, but still. He'd been suspended, and that was that.

Both of them were silent for a bit, and then he said, "Let's pray." Their agreement was whoever cooked, the other person prayed.

Gramps didn't say anything, just bowed his head.

"Lord God, please bless the food and keep it from killing us. Amen." That had been the gist of his prayer for the last week. So far, God had seen fit to answer with a yes.

Not that he was afraid to die, because he wasn't, he just didn't want to if it could be avoided for another half-century or so.

"Amen," Gramps echoed, and without any more conversation, they both dug into their food, knowing that if they didn't eat it, they were going to go to bed hungry.

The chicken was disgusting, dry on the inside and crispy/tough on the outside, but the view of the lake was beautiful, the breeze calming with the way it bent the grasses and rippled the water. It smelled fresh and clean and was just cool enough to be refreshing without being chilling.

Just ten yards or so from their cabin, there was a steep drop of about five feet to the shore. The cabin beside his had a slightly steeper drop, and on down the beach the shore rose up in bluffs that overlooked the lake.

Wesley and Gramps had only been there for five days, and he hadn't made it to the little town that sat at the top of the bluffs, but he figured it was probably a pretty view. He had walked down along the lake to the pebble beach that was right beneath the bluffs, although he hadn't gone the day he had arrived. It sounded like there was some kind of party going on, and he wondered if maybe he had made a bad choice. Perhaps teens hung out here since it was so isolated. Possibly even gangs. Not that he was afraid, he just didn't want to be bothered. He was supposed to be working on his memoir.

He hadn't expected to have someone in the cabin beside his either. When he'd bought it, he hadn't even realized he was going to have a neighbor.

But she—he was pretty sure it was a woman—kept to herself, which was just fine by him.

"Why don't you get over and introduce yourself to the neighbor? Be neighborly. You ought to bake a pie and take it over. That's what your grandma would do."

He was going to say if Gramps baked the pie, he would take it over, but he didn't want to scare the neighbors away.

"I think the definition of being neighborly is to let people know if you like and appreciate them. If I were to bake a pie, they would get the exact wrong impression."

"Maybe I could get on that there computer thing and look up a video. That's what everybody else does."

"Then I would have to go to the store and buy all the ingredients, and that seems like an awful lot of work to put into something that probably isn't going to turn out very well. Plus, I'm supposed to be writing a book. I don't have time to bake pies."

"You have time for what you make time for," Gramps said, and if Wesley had heard that once growing up, he heard it a million times.

His mom hadn't been married when she got pregnant with him, and she dropped her baby off with her parents before she split.

She calmed down from her wild ways and now had a nice family in Tulsa, and now that he was a big superstar hockey player, she wouldn't mind having something to do with him, but she hadn't been interested his entire growing-up years, and he wasn't overly interested now.

"I think I better make time to write a book. If I want to keep playing hockey anyway."

"Is that what you want?" Gramps said, with a change of voice that so often happened with him. He'd be gruff and tough one minute and tender and compassionate the next. Gramps really was a softy on the inside, but his edges were a little bit rough. Wesley could relate.

"Yes," he promised, and then he continued, because it was Gramps. "I can't imagine my life without hockey. I don't want to imagine my life without hockey," he said, shrugging one shoulder as he stuffed another bite of chicken in his mouth. He hadn't intended to go on a diet and in fact probably shouldn't. He could stand to gain a few pounds after losing weight after his grandma's funeral. She was the one who had always fed them, made sure he was eating okay, and told him about the evils of fast food and take-out.

He smiled thinking about it. She had always cared about them. More than anything else in the world. They were her life.

It was...nice to have someone who truly cared and wanted the best for you, someone that you knew was always going to be on your team. That was Gram. Gramps too, but he was a little rougher about it. And he couldn't cook.

"All right then, I guess you need to write the book, but I'm not going to be the full-time chef. You'd think a fellow would get some sympathy after he loses his wife of sixty-four years, but no, now the kid wants me to cook on top of me dealing with my grief." Gramps used his fork to cut into one of the still-hard beans on his plate. "My dentures are never going to be the same."

"Maybe we could hire a cook."

"And where exactly would they stay?" Gramps asked reasonably.

There were two single beds in the cabin. One on one side of the room, one on the other. There was a bathroom in the back, a fairly large bathroom, which must have been a recent addition, since the siding in the back of the cabin didn't match the rest of it. They'd done it well, with a large tile shower, tile floor, and a double sink. The bathroom was actually his favorite part of the cabin. The rest of it was kind of run down.

Gramps had been a carpenter by trade, but that had been years ago. Wesley had worked for him through high school, in the spring and early summer when he wasn't playing hockey.

Still, he had a book to write first, and any cooking or carpentry had to wait.

"Did I ever mention that I failed composition in high school?"

"I was there, remember? You did take summer school, and I had to take time off work every day to drive you to the school for your classes, then go pick you up and take you back to work with me. Do you think I'd forget something as inconvenient as that?" Gramps gave up on the fork, set it on the banister, and picked the beans up with his fingers. Wesley could hear them crunching on the other side of the porch where he sat.

Or maybe that was just his dentures flapping. He wasn't sure.

"How am I supposed to write a book when I couldn't even pass high school composition?"

"You managed to pass in college."

"That was because I had a girlfriend to write my papers for me." Wesley looked across the porch at Gramps and lifted his shoulder.

"She didn't write them for you; she helped you with them. There is a difference," Gramps said. But he continued to look at Wesley, as though waiting for Wesley to confirm what he'd always said.

"All right. You're right. I couldn't cheat. Because that would have been wrong, but I needed a lot of help, and she wasn't really my girlfriend."

"I know. You were just doing her a favor, increasing her prestige or whatever on campus by supposedly dating the big up-and-coming hockey player, and she returned the favor by helping you with your composition class."

Wesley nodded, wondering how much more of the chicken he could shove down and taking a big swig of his lemon water.

He had actually been the one to proposition the girl. She had thought he was going to do something lascivious and had shut him down right away, and then, when he had gotten to the meat of the issue, she laughed and said that she never thought of doing anything like that, but it might be fun.

She was shy and a little quiet, and by the time they had amicably "broken up," she had ended up being elected their college class president.

He was pretty sure she was having a fairly successful life in state politics, and it wouldn't shock him if she ended up on the national stage at some point. She had been a good girl. Totally refusing to do any kind of cheating, which he'd never asked her to do anyway, but completely willing to tutor him.

And to pretend to be his girlfriend.

He couldn't remember her name off the top of his head, but it had been one of the more fun memories he had of college.

"Maybe the girl over there knows how to cook," Gramps said. "Maybe I could...offer to fix that squeaky screen door of hers in return for a meal."

"Why don't you just leave her alone? She probably wants privacy just as much as we do." And he didn't want to risk her recognizing him or her being interested in some kind of relationship. He didn't have time for either one.

As he was thinking that, a sleek, shiny red sports car motored down the road, pulling in at the cabin beside theirs.

For a moment, Wesley had been afraid he'd been found out, but thankfully whoever was in the car was visiting the neighbors. Unless they had gotten the wrong cottage, which made Wesley want to jump up and run inside. But that would only bring more attention to him, so he sat still, like a rabbit trying not to be seen in the bushes.

"Maybe our neighbor got tired of trying to cook for herself and hired a chef. I wonder if she'd share?" Gramps said, looking curiously at the car as it pulled to a stop.

They waited for a few seconds, and then the driver's door opened. Wesley was almost holding his breath, which was the first time that he realized that perhaps he was a little bit understimulated at the cabin since nothing exciting had happened since they had come, other than the thrice daily burning of a meal. Once, his pork chops had caught on fire and he'd been a little concerned that he might burn the cabin down, but it had quickly been extinguished and was hardly worth mentioning.

A lady, older sixties, early seventies perhaps, stepped out of the car, standing up and looking around, her gaze catching on their porch for just a second before she looked straight ahead at the cottage beside them.

She reached in the car, pulled out a purse, slung it over her shoulder, and then backed up enough to shut the door. She wasn't dressed anything like his grandma, although she must have been about the same age.

"Yeah. I am definitely going to have to make a visit to the neighbor's house now. Can you think of anything else other than the squeaky screen door I could use as an excuse?"

Wesley rolled his eyes. Gramps was just joking. He would never love anyone the way he'd loved Gram, but things had definitely gotten a lot more interesting around here in the last five minutes.

Birdie Pollock looked around the cabin in which she spent the last five days. It looked a lot better than it had when she arrived, when there had been dusty cobwebs everywhere, broken boards, and debris on the floor.

It didn't exactly look like a home, yet. But she was working on it.

Which was a really nice way to keep her mind off the pressures of her job. She used to love to sing, but now, singing was just as much of a job to her as if she'd become an accountant like her parents wanted her to.

She still felt tired, exhausted, with the bone-deep exhaustion that felt like sleep couldn't even touch. But with enough rest and relaxation, she was confident she could overcome it and be ready to go back to work by October.

The sound of a sports car came through the screen door, and she figured that either the neighbors had gotten a new car, or her gram had arrived.

She hadn't counted on having neighbors. The cabin beside hers had not been shown in any of the pictures that she'd seen.

Regardless, they had left her alone, and as far as she knew, they just thought she was an ordinary citizen. Her haircut and color change had done the trick.

Of course, her roots would soon be growing out, and she would have to make the decision as to whether or not she was going to dye it again or take a chance of someone recognizing her.

She also was about ready to make a grocery run, and she needed to figure out whether she was going to change her name or continue to use Birdie. It wasn't exactly a common name, but she knew several people who had it as a nickname.

Drying her hands off on a tea towel, she carefully set it over the handle of the oven, which, now that her grandma was here, would most certainly be in use, and stepped to the screen door.

Her gram hadn't changed a bit. The car was parked crooked and at least five feet away from the end of the parking space.

She probably shouldn't have rented a Ferrari for her, but...she couldn't resist the temptation. She smiled, knowing that was the exact reason why she'd done it—it would be amusing. Both for Gram and for herself.

As her gram got out of the car and stood looking around at the cottage, Birdie pushed the screen door open and stepped out on the porch, careful not to allow it to slam behind her. How many times growing up had she heard her grandma say, "Birdie, don't let that screen door slam!"

She'd even been made to come back and close it quietly. Now, thanks to her gram, it was habit to shut the door quietly every time.

"Birdie! You didn't tell me you had neighbors. It's a good thing I brought my pie fixins."

She grinned, shaking her head. She'd been brought up in a small town in Arkansas with her dad and her gram. Her mom had died shortly after childbirth from a ruptured aneurysm, and in order to have his mom watch her, her dad had moved back in with his parents.

His dad passed away before she had any cognizant memories of him, but her gram colored her childhood with beautiful, happy, homelike memories. Pies were just one of the many things that she remembered her gram pulling out of the oven that smelled divine and made their house a home. Good food along with copious amounts of love and goodwill had made it so that most of the time she didn't remember she didn't have a mother. Her gram was a positive thinker before it became popular. In fact, it wouldn't shock Birdie to find out she penned the word.

"I'm sorry." Her gram was digging in the back for things to carry in, and Birdie stepped off the porch, walking to the car to give her a hand.

Her gram was not afraid to delegate, and stood up, unsurprised to see her granddaughter standing in front of her, and loaded her down with bags of flour, sugar, a bucket of blueberries she probably picked on her way here, pie plates, and a bag of ingredients that probably came from whatever box store Gram had passed. She certainly wouldn't pay full price at a regular grocery store.

"My goodness, you look white as a ghost, and you've lost weight since I've seen you last." Her gram straightened again, wrapping her arms around her, bags dangling from her hands as she encompassed Birdie and all the things that she'd given her to carry. "I'm here now, so I can get started taking care of you."

"You know, Gram. I am an adult."

"I know. And you've been an adult for ten or fifteen years now, but that doesn't mean that I can't still take care of you."

She had no idea where her gram got her energy. It seemed like there were boundless amounts that just flowed from her. Anytime there was a need, her gram was the first to jump in to help. She had no idea what her small Arkansas town was going to do without her for several months.

But this town, what was the name? Raspberry Ridge. That was it. She had a friend here, Olive, who had extolled its virtues—quiet, small, and beautiful. They were all true. Anyway, this town would definitely benefit from having her gram around, as would her neighbors.

"So, once we get settled, you're going to have to introduce me to your neighbors. Let me make a pie first, so I can take it over—"

"I actually haven't met the neighbors yet," she said as they climbed the stairs. She happened to notice that the neighbors were both out on their porch, staring at the newcomers. Until her gram had waved excitedly, the way one might wave if one was starving in the desert dying of thirst and happened to see a freight train coming through.

Birdie closed her eyes. So many times during her childhood, her grandma had embarrassed her by her over-friendliness toward anyone, friends, family, coworkers, acquaintances, and complete strangers. Her grandma never met someone she didn't consider an immediate friend.

Birdie wasn't sure how she did it, but she had gone from enjoying it as a child, to being embarrassed by it as a teen, to admiring and appreciating it as an adult. Except, right now. She didn't really want visitors.

"Gram. I'm not really up to that right now. I'm here because I need to get away from everyone, not make new best friends."

"Of course we're not going to make best friends, honey, but friends are friends, and you can never have too many,"

She admired her gram, but she did disagree about that. She couldn't keep track of too many friends. She preferred to have just three or four close friends and really dig deep, being the very best friend that she could and knowing that they would be there for her no matter what.

Her gram was the exact opposite, a lot of surface friends, and while Gram was always up for a deep discussion and a piece of pie, she had way too many friends to be able to do that with the time and depth Birdie would prefer.

She sometimes felt like Gram brushed her off, only giving her the perfunctory amount of time before running off to throw a piece of pie and some advice at someone else.

She knew that wasn't true and that Gram did her best. Possibly it had taken her until the last few years to realize that it was just Gram's personality and not a character flaw on either her part or her gram's. They had different philosophies, different personalities, and different ways they viewed the world and lived in it. She liked to go quiet and deep. Gram liked to be loud and spread out. Both ways were okay. Because God had designed them both.

Some people said introvert and extrovert, which probably summed it up just as well.

Funny that a world-famous singer could be such a huge introvert. But that was probably why she was struggling so hard with her fame. She'd had a more demanding concert schedule this year than she had in the previous ten, and while it had been extremely profitable, it had almost broken her.

"You have a little bit of time, because it's gonna take me a bit to bake a pie. Did you get the place cleaned up?" Gram asked as Birdie opened the door to hold it for her gram while she walked in. It was kind of hard to balance all of the things in her arms, but she used her foot to push it open and then caught it with her hip, balancing the top pie plate with her chin.

"I've done what I could. I haven't wanted to go to town."

"Why ever not, child? It's obvious this place needs some curtains, some Windex, and paper towels?"

Paper towels were a luxury that she hadn't used when she was a child, but her grandma got addicted to them when she decided that they were biodegradable and hence good for the environment.

"No. I didn't bring paper towels, I...thought the cabin was going to be in a little better shape."

The problem was she was used to the luxury accommodations she normally had on tour. Her booking agent had not booked this place. She had done it herself. She actually had her booking agent book her a place in Switzerland, which was where the world was supposed to think she was.

She hadn't checked any social media sites to see if there were any reports of any Birdie sightings in Switzerland or Europe.

"That's okay. I'm here now, and you can just rest until your little soul is happy. I'll have this place whipped up into shape in no time. Except... I am a terrible painter, and those walls need to be painted bad." Her gram stood for a second, hand on her chin looking at the walls. They were bare wood and almost looked like they'd been made from driftwood. Perhaps they had. Regardless, they were a nasty brownish gray color, which was natural and perhaps even pleasing to some folks, but her gram liked blocks of color.

"Can we paint them pink and white? I think it would make it feel brighter in here if the colors on the walls weren't so dark."

"Or a nice creamy yellow would be cheerful. Like lemons."

Lemons were better than apples. She couldn't stand red. The entire house had been red when she had been a kid, and she had liked it okay, but it felt like an angry color, like blood and all of that. "Maybe a nice pleasing purple?" she asked, knowing that her gram absolutely hated purple.

"What about turquoise? Kind of goes with the seashore theme."

"Can we do accents in turquoise?"

And then she wondered why in the world she was even arguing about this. She didn't care what color Gram painted the cabin, or if she even painted it at all. She just knew that Gram would keep it clean, and she would definitely keep food on the table, which...might be a bit of a problem since her appetite still had not come back. She expected after five days that she would be mostly better, more energy, her thinking more clear with an appetite, but not yet.

"All right. Well, I'll get started with the list, and then I'm gonna send you to town with it, and after that, you can sleep the rest of the day." She held her hand up, apparently just in case Birdie was going to revert to her teenage years in protest. "And I will get started whipping this place into shape. I'm sure you've done a great job, but a lot of improvements remain to be made," she said, looking over the glasses that perched on the end of her nose as she made another slow twirl around the room.

"What did you think of your car?" Birdie asked, knowing that a trip to town was inevitable. She wasn't going to tell her gram no, although if she did, her gram would never make her go, would go for her. But even though she was supposed to be resting and recovering, this was still a two-way street, and she wasn't just going to dump all the work on her gram.

"My goodness." Her gram stopped and grinned. "I laughed when I saw it, because the lady at the counter said that you had left a note that I was to get a specific car." Her gram rolled her eyes. "I thought it might have been a minivan, since you had never been able to get me into one of those crazy contraptions, but it was even worse."

For as long as she'd known her gram, she'd driven as big of a car as she could get. She said they were safer. Which, technically she was correct, but her preference nowadays was a big SUV, which came in handy anytime the Ozarks got snow in the winter.

"I figured you'd get a laugh out of it, and I enjoyed seeing you pull up in it too."

It had been fun, and as she thought, her gram thought it was funny as well. She hadn't been able to get the model where the doors opened up, but still, just seeing her gram drive a sports car had been worth it.

"I just hope we're not here come winter, because that thing is going to go like a sled in the snow."

"It's so flat here. It won't go anywhere in the snow. It'll just sit and spin."

"Regardless, it will be worthless from about November to March."

"It might even be longer than that here as far north as we are."

"I can't argue about that. But I did enjoy driving it from the airport. There just weren't any fun corners to speed around."

"If that were the case, I wouldn't have rented it, because I figured you would be tempted along those lines."

They laughed together. Her gram was known as a speed demon, even in the large SUVs she drove. Birdie had always been the more conscientious of the two of them.

"So what's the church like here?" her gram asked as she carefully removed some things from the bag. Then, apparently thinking better of it, she grabbed a rag and started scrubbing the counters.

"I didn't go on Sunday."

"You didn't go?" Her gram stopped scrubbing and turned around, giving her an all-too-familiar look over the top rim of her glasses.

"Gram, I'm supposed to be resting and recovering, not running around socializing."

"Church is not a social organization. Sure, we have fellowship with believers, but it's for more than that. You go to worship God, and you go to hear God's word preached, because all of us need that shot in the arm at least once a week. Do they have a Wednesday night service?"

"They do." Her words were cautious, because she could almost hear what was coming next.

"All right. Then let's plan on going tomorrow evening."

"All right. Let's plan on going." She wasn't going to mention that Olive had told her there was a daily Bible study every morning except Sunday on somebody's front porch right on Main Street. The second her gram knew about that, they'd be going with bells on. And taking enough food to feed an entire village when they did it. And unless her grandma lost her touch, they'd be dragging the neighbors along with them.

All Birdie knew about the neighbors was that they were two men. She hadn't tried to look at them to see if she recognized them or even to do more than throw up a hand in a wave as she walked inside. She wanted to be friendly, but friendly as in waving a hand at the neighbors, not friendly as in actually talking to them. First of all, she didn't want them to recognize her, and secondly, she wanted to be able to rest and recuperate and not be forced into a conversation every time she left her house.

Of course, not everyone viewed the idea of being forced into a conversation with as much loathing as what she did.

She put the groceries her grandma had brought away and was thinking about grabbing her notebook and going out to sit on the beach for a while. She wrote all of her own songs and typically tried to carry a notebook wherever she went, in case inspiration struck. Inspiration had been very sketchy lately, and she didn't have a single song for her new album that was supposed to release just a few weeks before her tour started.

October was supposed to be spent in the recording booth, putting the new songs together for an album.

She wasn't exactly pressed for time, but typically she had all of her songs written by now and had so many she was trying to weed out which ones she wanted to keep and which ones she wanted to go.

But she probably should focus on getting the things they needed before she allowed herself to sink into a creative state.

"If you can think of anything else you need, don't be afraid to pick it up. This place is bare-bones, but we can fix that."

"Okay," she said, knowing it was pointless to argue. Plus, it was almost seven o'clock, and since the closest grocery store was Blueberry Beach, it would be at least nine o'clock before she got back. By then, she would be more than ready to head to bed.

"Gram?" Birdie stood in front of the screen door with the list in her hand, her eyes serious.

Gram saw her expression and paused from where she had found a piece of steel wool and was scrubbing at the stove. "What is it?"

"Please remember that I'm not anything here but just me." Her gram had never been big on the big star popularity/everyone knew her name kind of thing, but she had gone to some of her concerts and traveled with her a bit and knew that she was a bit of a big deal, worldwide.

"I know. You don't want people to know you, so the people who take all the pictures and have the cameras and try to spy on your every move won't find out where you are and bother us." She paused for a moment, then her eyes scrunched down and she looked at the windows. "But I think I can get some pretty nice curtains snapped together in a little bit of time, and they'll never be able to—"

"Just... It would be better if they didn't find out I was here to begin with."

"If I get my pie made and taken over to the neighbors, I can guarantee you that I won't say a word about you." Her gram nodded her head, gave her a little smile, and then went back to scrubbing the stove. "Unless they ask, and then you know I can't lie."

Her grandma was a talker, and sometimes she did say things she shouldn't, but Birdie knew that if she said she wasn't going to mention that Birdie was a big singer, she wouldn't. It wasn't like her gram to brag anyway. She'd never heard her introduce her like that anywhere. In fact, she wasn't even sure why she had worried about it. She just...wanted some peace and quiet. But she also didn't want to have to cook for herself, so she definitely appreciated her gram coming.

"I'm going to borrow your car, Gram," she said with a grin as she walked out the door.

"That's fine. You just drive it like it's yours," Gram called after her.

Three

"What did I tell you?" Gramps said as he stood at the window, peeking out through the one spot that they'd rubbed a circle of dirt off so they could see out.

Wesley knew he probably should figure out whatever kind of cleaner people used to clean windows and use it on theirs, but he hadn't been inspired to do that. Instead, he'd been so uptight about writing the book that he should have had written a year ago but he had kept putting off. There wasn't any reason for him to have not started it. It was all Wesley's fault.

"What did you tell me?" Wesley got up from where he was writing at the small table, or staring at the blank screen with his fingers poised above the keyboard, and walked over to the window.

"I think she's carrying a pie!" Gramps said, and he couldn't keep the excitement out of his voice.

It was true that sometimes he put a little weight on in the off-season, but not this year. So far, he'd been staying in shape by taking long runs on the beach and doing all the exercises he knew to do without machines, but he probably should hit the gym. He didn't want to come in in the middle of the season out of shape.

Regardless, whether he was underweight or working on losing

some, he could count on one hand the number of times he'd had homemade pie, and he was pretty sure that being that the lady was holding it with oven mitts on both hands, this one had just come out of the oven.

"I think we had an angel move in next door," Gramps said.

"I think you're being a little melodramatic. Don't scare her away on her first trip. There might be more than pie in her repertoire, and it would be a shame if we didn't get to try it all."

Gramps gave him a grin, like they were conspiring to be nice to their neighbors just for personal gain, when both of them knew that not to be true. If the lady hadn't come over this evening, Gramps would have found a reason to go visit the next day, and not just because he was hoping she would cook for them. Although, he definitely was not going to turn food down. Neither of them would, after the "food" they'd been eating for the last five days.

"I think I better go offer to carry it for her," Gramps said as he hurried toward the door. He was in his late seventies but was still just as spry as he was when he was fifty.

"If you're going to carry it for her, you might want to think of something to protect your hands. She's wearing oven mitts."

"Good thinking, boy. I knew I raised you right." Gramps turned from the door and searched for something he could use.

"Here." Wesley threw him the first thing he could grab, and Gramps caught it as it hit his chest.

"An old T-shirt?" Gramps questioned. Then he lifted his shoulder, turned, and went out the door.

Wesley shook his head. He probably should forget about getting anything done, other than writing the words "Chapter 1" at the top of the screen. Which he had already done six months ago when he realized that he needed to get on this. But he didn't know where to start. Did he start with his childhood? His birth? Could he explain all the things that had gone on? Or were readers just interested in hockey? Should he start with his first professional game? It seemed like his life had been predestined long before his first professional hockey game. But he didn't know what else to do.

He still hadn't figured anything out when Gramps came back in the house, one hand underneath the pie, one hand opening and closing the door.

"It's blueberry," he said, like he was announcing the birth of the long-awaited heir to the kingdom.

"Blueberry is my favorite. You probably ought to let me eat it."

"Everything is your favorite. She made me promise to share with you, but that does not include allowing you to have the entire thing," his gramps said, lifting his brows and giving him a warning look. A look that Wesley understood to mean that he was only going to get half of the pie. If that. "If you wanted more, you should have gone out to meet her."

"Did you talk her into cooking breakfast for us tomorrow?"

"Baby steps, son. Baby steps." Gramps held up a hand as he set the pie down on the counter. "We're invited over for supper tomorrow night."

"That's awesome. Are you serious?"

"I sure am. Chicken divan. Her secret family recipe. Apparently she's there with her granddaughter, who happens to be a writer."

"A writer? Are you serious?"

"When I asked her what her granddaughter did, she said she was a writer."

"That's awesome. Maybe..."

"I already know what you're thinking, and I think if we work our cards right, we just might have hit the jackpot with our neighbors."

"Are you sure you don't need me for anything else?" Birdie stood at the door, her notebook in her hand. She helped her gram clean the house this morning, then they'd both taken a rest before Gram had gotten up and started getting ready to make supper for their neighbors this evening. Birdie should have known better than to leave her alone for even two seconds, or their house would be filled with people. Not that she normally minded, but... Maybe it wasn't such a good idea to have Gram here. But when she told Gram that she was going up and Gram was welcome to join her, she hadn't realized there was going to be another cottage right next door.

"No. You go on out and write another one of your hit songs. Oh, that reminds me, when I went over yesterday to take them the pie, they asked me what you do for a living."

A sinking feeling dragged Birdie's stomach down to her kneecaps. "And what did you tell them?"

"I told him you were a writer. You're always running around with a notebook and pen in your hand, so it's obvious that that's what you are." Her gram laughed. "I thought it was clever. Go ahead. You can tell me I was clever. It's okay."

"Actually, that is kind of clever, Gram. Thanks for not giving away anything else."

"You can sit at the table tonight and police me, give me the hairy eyeball if I say anything you don't approve of."

"Oh, you know I will," she said before she pushed the door open and stepped out into the bright afternoon sunlight. There was almost always a breeze from the lake, which kept things from getting too warm. If she had to guess, the temperature was probably in the high seventies. Not a bad day for Northern Michigan.

She went down the steps to the beach and out until she was at the edge of the dry sandy pebbles. The lake was rather calm, with small waves crashing against the shore. Just enough to give it the sound that she loved, without the dangerous undertow. Not that she had any plans of getting in the water. She could swim, but not well. And typically she stayed out of any area where it might be the slightest bit dangerous. She didn't enjoy swimming well enough to risk her life for it.

She'd been sitting there for twenty minutes and had one word written in her notebook—peace—before she saw what looked like a head bobbing in the waves down the beach.

She shaded her eyes to get a better look, thinking that it might be someone who needed help, although they had been in the water for a while, since she hadn't seen anyone either up or down the beach in the amount of time that she'd been out there. But as she looked, she realized it was a man swimming.

She'd seen her neighbor go out to swim once or twice since she'd gotten there, but that had always been in the early morning.

But as he drew closer, he started to come nearer to the shore, and she realized that regardless of when his previous outings had been, he'd chosen to take a swim this afternoon.

She looked back down at her notebook, willing the words to come into her head but unable to think of anything.

Still, she couldn't stare at her neighbor as he got out of the water and walked up the beach, about fifty yards from her. She lifted her head once, threw up a hand and waved, and looked back down without checking to see whether he had returned her wave or not.

She'd done the friendly thing. But she felt guilty about it. Maybe that was part of her problem. Maybe rather than being isolated from people, she should embrace them, get involved in the town, and live a normal life. Maybe the two extremes, one extreme of being around screaming fans for three hours each evening, then driving or flying for another eight to twelve hours to the next venue, versus being by herself in an isolated cabin along Lake Michigan... Maybe neither one of those were the way to go. Maybe she needed more moderation.

Well, they were having guests over for supper tonight, so that was a beginning. And Gram was going to make sure they went to church tomorrow evening, so there was another beginning. And if she knew her gram, she would sign up for every volunteer spot available where they would allow a nonmember to participate. And if they wouldn't allow nonmembers, Gram would join.

Birdie wasn't entirely sure she was up for all of that, but maybe a little bit would be helpful. She had enjoyed working with her gram this morning and felt better than she had in a while.

She couldn't even think of how long, since she'd been so tired for the last leg of her tour, she had just been getting through it through sheer willpower and determination.

When sitting in the sand for another thirty minutes did not give her any more words on her paper, she got up and took a short walk, thinking that maybe moving her body would help. But it didn't, and "peace" was the only thing she had written down by the time she came back to the cottage and walked in.

"Did you have a good walk?" her gram asked, apron around her waist, eyeglasses on her nose, and flour on both hands.

"I did. I figured I'd come in and see what I can do to help."

"You can set the table. I saw some wildflowers outside there earlier. We could pick some to make a little bouquet, which would make the table a little more cheerful. I'm going to get some color on these walls, just mark my words. I hate to do it though because there's a couple of spots that need to be fixed and all the window frames need to be replaced. The wood is rotted."

She hadn't even noticed the rotted wood. Which went to show how much attention she'd been paying to the finer points of the cabin. She just wanted a clean place to lay her head. And food to eat. That was kind of important. Clean dishes maybe.

Dutifully she set the table as neatly as she'd been taught and walked outside to pick flowers. She was on her way back in with the flowers when she saw her neighbors leaving their cottage.

"They're on their way," she announced as she came in, grabbing a mason jar because they didn't have a vase and filling it up with water from the kitchen sink.

"Thanks for the warning, and it's perfect timing," Gram said, looking at her watch. "4:58. I like a man who can be on time."

She hadn't heard her gram talk about what she liked in a man for a long time. She had gotten the feeling that her gram and pap's relationship hadn't been the best, as he had not been a very good husband, but she never got the details from Gram. She kind of figured Gram thought she was too young to know, and then as she got older, she'd gotten involved in her career and all the things she needed to do to make it work and grow, and she hadn't asked anymore.

"So you have a type?" she asked, smiling a little because she was teasing.

"I don't know that I have a type, but a guy who can be on time is a bit of a treasure. In my experience, it's always the man that makes the family late."

"Well, you have more experience than I do with that," she said calmly. "But it looks like this guy is going to be on time. At least one of them got them both out the door early."

She figured it could have been the swimmer who pushed the older man out.

"Did you find out if it was a grandfather with his grandson?"

"I didn't ask. I just gave him the pie and talked about the weather for a little bit and he asked about us. I was so pleased with myself for being clever that I didn't carry the conversation any further and simply said good night."

"It looks like they have your empty pie pan," Birdie said as she watched them climb the steps to the porch

"Land sakes!" her gram said, peering out the screen door and then turning wide eyes onto Birdie. "I wasn't expecting that."

"Knock, knock," a voice called.

Birdie didn't have to tell them to come in, she was standing right there.

Opening the door, she said, "Welcome. So glad you could make it. I'm Birdie." The younger man walked in first, and she suppressed a sting of disappointment. His T-shirt stretched tight over a wide chest and bulged over defined biceps. Obviously he was a guy who spent a lot of time in the gym, and in Birdie's experience, guys who were gym rats were often boring. All they wanted to do was talk about nutrition and their muscles. In fact, they typically had never seen a mirror they didn't love to stand and preen in front of.

She spent enough time with guys like that that she had started avoiding them.

Of course, she knew she was judging, and she tried to push all that aside, but her perfect smile was forced as he shook her hand and said, "I'm Wes."

"Good to meet you, Wes. You've already met my grandmother."

"And this is my grandfather, Gramps. He has a name, but no one ever uses it."

"All right then. Good to meet you, Gramps," she said gamely. It was weird assigning such a familiar name to someone she'd never met before, but she could do it.

"Should I call your gram Gram?"

"What do you think about that, Gram?" she asked, figuring she wasn't the one who needed to say. Although people at church usually called her Mrs. Pollock, there were other people who called her Polly, her given name.

"Gram is fine, if that makes you comfortable," Gram said with an easy, welcoming smile. "Just let me get this flour rinsed off my hands. I put the cinnamon rolls in the oven, and they should be piping hot and ready by the time we're done eating."

"I brought the blueberry pie pan back, and I was hoping you'd have something more for dessert tonight." Gramps waved the pie pan around like a white flag of surrender. Or maybe a red flag in front of the bull, which would probably be a more apt description of Gram, if not the pie plate.

"Oh my goodness, that disappeared fast," Gram said, wiping her hands and taking the pie plate away from him.

"It was the best pie I'd ever eaten. Regardless of the kind."

"Blueberry is my favorite, and I admit I had almost half of it."

"Almost half, is that so," Gram said, looking at Wes before turning back to Gramps. "So that means, if my math is correct, you ate a little over half."

"And I cherished every bite. It almost makes a man want to pledge to keep you supplied in blueberries for the summer if you'll keep him supplied in blueberry pie."

"Well, there are other kinds of pie that are almost as good," Gram said, then she added, "But if you want to keep me supplied in blueberries, I'm pretty sure I can find a little bit of time in my day to make blueberry pie anytime I have some extra blueberries sitting around."

"That's a deal," Gramps said.

They shifted a bit, looking at the table. Birdie figured that it was her turn to try to be a good hostess, and she said, "Would you like to sit down? We're ready to put the food on the table. Gram made our family's famous chicken divan, and we've never had anyone who has eaten and not loved it."

"I'm looking forward to it. Although I have to say, as long as it's not burnt and not raw, I'm pretty sure it's going to be better than anything we've had for the last six days."

"You fellas can't cook?" Gram said, and if she hadn't had the chicken divan in her hands, she might have been rubbing them together. Birdie could almost see her thinking of all the things that she could make for their new neighbors. Anyone who appreciated her cooking was a lifelong friend to Gram. Of course, Birdie couldn't talk, because she definitely appreciated her gram's cooking. She hadn't inherited her abilities, although she could make food that would keep her from starving.

They finished setting the food on the table, and it did smell delicious. Her walk had given her a bit of an appetite, since it had been a while since food even smelled good to her. She hoped she was able to eat enough so she didn't draw attention to herself. She didn't want anyone looking at her and wondering why she wasn't eating.

As they settled in their chairs, Gram looked over at Gramps and said, "Would you like to say grace for us?"

This always made Birdie hold her breath. There had been multiple times they had invited people over to eat who had acted surprised or offended that they said grace before their meal and even more surprised and offended when they had been asked to say it for them.

Personally, Birdie thought it was probably a good idea that if they were going to invite guests over, they should be the ones planning on saying grace. But her gram was old-fashioned that way and did not say a prayer if there was a man around to say it for her.

Birdie knew that the Bible said that it was a shame for women to speak in church, but there wasn't anything that said a woman couldn't say grace in her own house. Regardless, she didn't argue with her gram about it. She could handle it however she wanted to. Birdie just thought it would make their guests more comfortable to not put them on the spot like that.

But to her surprise, Gramps nodded immediately. "I'd love to. Especially when it smells like this."

They all bowed their heads, and Gramps began, "Lord God, thank you for food that smells like it's not just going to be edible but delicious. I pray that You bless it, bless our conversation, and bless this lady's hands, and make them literally fruitful all summer long. Amen."

Birdie smothered a smile before she looked up. She was pretty sure that Gramp's prayer was...deliberately humorous.

In an underhanded sort of way. The kind of humor that she knew Gram could get on board with. Gram might be an in-your-face person, but she and Birdie got along well, because they were opposites. Gramps seemed a little bit more outgoing than Birdie, but his humor seemed a little understated, perfect to complement her gram.

And there she was, all of a sudden she'd gone from pop superstar to matchmaker. When had she ever been interested in matchmaking her gram?

She'd always been selfish and wanted her gram for herself. This could end up being an interesting summer.

"So, Birdie, that's a unique name," Gramps said as he helped himself to a piece of chicken.

"My mom was a unique person," she said, her standard answer for such a thing.

"Your gram said when she was over yesterday, that you were a writer. You write books?" Wes spoke as he took the pan of chicken from his grandfather.

Boy. What to say about that. Gram and her clever answer. She looked over, and Gram met her eyes, an apology on her face. Birdie couldn't be upset with her. She was just trying to be friendly. And she would never ask her to lie. So, saying that she was a writer was better than saying that she was a pop sensation superstar, world-famous and getting ready to gear up for her Asian tour which started in January of the next year.

"I haven't written a book yet," she said, smiling. And then, so he couldn't ask a follow-up question, she reached over to take the chicken divan from him and said, "But Gram didn't say what you did for a living?"

She figured, from the look of it, he was probably some kind of athletic instructor or something along those lines.

"I'm actually writing a book too."

"Oh," she said, truly surprised. That was not what she was expecting at all.

She tried to find the smallest piece of chicken in the dish, hoping that Gram had maybe cut one in half thinking of her, but no such luck.

She got the least amount that she was able to take and set it on her plate. She hadn't eaten that much in months. There was no way she was going to shovel that entire piece down her throat, and the side salad and rolls hadn't even passed her yet.

Not that she was hungry for either of those things either.

The sticky buns smelled good though. Maybe she just needed some carbs.

"What kind of books are you writing?" she asked as she passed the chicken on to her gram and took the rolls from Wes.

"I'm writing a nonfiction book." He sounded like he might want to say more, but he clamped his mouth closed. As though he felt like he couldn't trust her. She almost laughed. So she wasn't the only one keeping secrets. She wondered what in the world kind of nonfiction book he could be writing. A book on all the exercises a person could do with just a lake and a cottage and a beach?

"I used to be a carpenter. And I happened to notice that your window frames could be replaced. I don't want to brag on myself, but I used to do pretty good work. I was wondering if you might want to trade window frames for food?" Gramps looked at Gram when he said that.

As well he should, since Birdie certainly wasn't the one who had made the delicious food. At least from the way it smelled, she assumed it was delicious. She'd gotten one bite in her mouth, but it just tasted like shredded paper to her. She knew her appetite would come back, but she just needed to give it time.

She sighed, because that seemed to be what everything took, time, right? She tried not to be discouraged. It was going to take time to write songs for her album, time for her to feel better, time for her life to pan out the way she wanted it to.

She hadn't planned on being a pop superstar, and she couldn't complain, because so many people would kill to be in her position, but she wanted a normal life too. Kids, husband, a family. The kind of childhood she remembered growing up at her grandma's house.

"Well, I was going to give you food whether you traded me anything for it or not, but I certainly am not going to turn down having the window frames replaced."

Gram didn't mention it, but Birdie had not rented the cottage. She'd leased it first, then persuaded the owner to sell. The papers hadn't been signed yet. They were just waiting for the closing date. Everything had been drawn up.

"You don't need to check with the landlord?" Wes asked, lifting a brow and almost sounding like he was suspicious of something.

"We own the house." She didn't say anything more. She wanted to explain, just in case he had owned his house for years and knew the neighbors. She might as well not sit around and wonder about it, but just go ahead and ask.

"How long have you lived in your cottage?" she asked, assuming that that wasn't their permanent residence. It must get pretty wicked in the winter.

"We just moved in. Five days ago, actually, six counting today. Wes here bought it and decided it would make a nice—"

Wes gave Gramps a look, and Gramps's mouth clamped closed faster than the blueberry pie had disappeared.

Interesting. Very, very interesting.

Five

"Nice, so you and Gramps own your cottage as well?" Gram said, and maybe she didn't feel the tension on the other side of the table. Wes knew his gramps was just doing his best to make conversation and also to secure food so that the two of them didn't starve, but he hadn't wanted them to know that they had money.

Of course, Birdie didn't exactly look comfortable with his line of questioning either. He guessed that both of them had things that they didn't want the other one to know.

Honestly, he wanted to be able to allow her to keep her secrets. But he also wanted to be able to keep his.

"We did. It's pretty run down, and I'm sure you know it wasn't that expensive." That wasn't entirely true. It wasn't expensive compared to the other houses down near Strawberry Sands and Blueberry Beach where it was more industrialized and touristy. However, Raspberry Ridge was the next place those places would expand, and prices were going up.

He hadn't even considered the bottom line, just bought the house because they needed it.

Still, the idea that she was a writer was interesting, and he wanted to talk more about that. Even if she couldn't write his book for him, maybe she could help him with it.

"So how long have you been writing?" he asked, taking another bite and managing not to close his eyes and groan. This was the best food he'd had in a long time. Gram was definitely a good cook. And he didn't want to stand in Gramps's way if he was going to be able to get her to cook for them. He just didn't want the entire world to know that he was here. But maybe once he got to know Birdie, he could tell her who he was. If she was going to help him with his story, he was going to have to admit his identity or act like he was writing a biography of a current professional hockey player.

"I've been writing all my life. I wrote little short poems when I was a kid, and... Yeah. I just do more short form than books."

"I see." Maybe she wouldn't be a help after all. "If you'd like to spend some time writing together, we could meet on the beach at some point. I don't know about you, but I've been struggling with a major case of writer's block." A block that had never been removed, since he had never been very good at writing.

"That's funny. I've been struggling with writer's block myself." She paused, pushing the chicken that she had cut up around on her plate. He hadn't seen her take more than one bite. Not that he was paying a lot of attention, she just...seemed skinny. "I wouldn't mind meeting on the beach and trying to write."

"Maybe I can give you some ideas for yours, and you can give me some ideas for mine."

"Maybe we could."

They were all quiet for a few minutes, but Wesley barely noticed. He didn't think he was wrong that Birdie would rather they not know, but she also seemed...familiar, in a haunting kind of way. He almost had a visceral reaction to her, which was unusual for him. Typically he avoided people, ducking away from them, not trying to look under the surface of the person he was talking to and figure them out. But that's how he felt about Birdie. Like there was a lot there, and he wanted to uncover it.

He tried to tell himself that there would be plenty of time for him to get to know her, since they were going to be meeting on the beach to write together.

"How long are you guys planning on staying? Is it your permanent home?" Gramps asked, scooping out his second helping of chicken divan.

"We're not to be here any later than the end of September," Gram said, and she sounded a little cagey. "What about you guys? How long am I going to be baking pies for you?" She added a little bit of humor to it, and it took some of the interrogation out of the question, but Wesley still felt like she was digging for information.

"We're only here until the end of September. Maybe less. We'll see," Gramps said.

"I would think that it would be pretty rough here in the winter, although it might be fun to be snowed in," Wes added to the conversation, although he knew that as long as he was playing hockey, there was no way he was going to be able to be here during the winter, not during the season.

"What kind of pies do you like to make?" Gramps asked Gram, taking another roll to go along with his second helping of chicken.

"I always make whatever fruit is in season. Right now, it's blueberry season here in Michigan, and the beginning of apple season."

"I love apple pies," Wesley interjected, figuring that if Gramps had seconds, he might as well too. Birdie was still pushing around the first chicken she'd gotten on her plate, and she'd broken her roll in half, but she hadn't eaten anything.

"I'll have to make sure you get plenty. The later apples are the better apples for pies. These first apples are great for applesauce and for just eating."

"You sound like you know a little bit of something about apples."

"I come from a family of farmers, and we had an orchard growing up."

"Where was that?" Gramps asked, sounding truly interested. Gramps had grown up on a farm as well, so that was probably where his interest came.

"The Ozarks. We have an apple down there called the Ozark Black. It's a dark red apple, deep, with a very tart taste. It makes delicious pies. I doubt I'll see it this far north," Gram said, taking a sip of her water. "But

I can probably make fair to middlin' pies with whatever I can find around here."

"What about pumpkin?" Wes asked, thinking of his second favorite pie.

"Pumpkin pies, minced meat pies, raspberry, strawberry, apple, blueberry, even sweet potato pies."

"My favorite are your potpies. The savory ones." Birdie spoke up. She hadn't said anything since they talked about her writing and how long they were going to be staying. That's when Birdie had clammed up, like she didn't want any of that information to get out.

Pies seemed like a safe subject, and one that Gramps enjoyed anyway.

"We'll make some of those too. I haven't forgotten that you love those."

"She makes them with cream, and they're so good."

"The secret ingredient is celery seeds. I'll swear by it. Even though most people wrinkle their noses when I tell them that."

"And thyme. You put thyme in them too."

"I wasn't going to tell them about that secret ingredient," Gram said, a little huffy, and Wesley almost believed that she had been going to keep that from them, like Gramps would have any idea of what thyme was or how to use it in a potpie.

"Sorry," Birdie said, grinning a bit, but her cheeks got red.

Gram had given her a look, and some kind of communication passed between the two women. If Wesley had to guess, he'd say that Birdie was saying "you had given away some of my information, but I didn't mean to give away any of yours," and Gram had forgiven her.

"After supper, Birdie and I are heading to church. It will be our first time there. But you're welcome to join us. I'm sure the whole community is welcome."

"That seems to be the thing with churches. They're always trying to get new members."

"They help bring in money," Gramps said, and he didn't exactly sound bitter, but he did sound a little annoyed. Wesley tried not to cringe. The church had not been very good to him when his wife died.

They brought a couple of meals and basically said "she was a great woman, see you later."

Wesley wasn't quite sure what exactly Gramps expected the church to do, but he expected a little bit more than a casserole and a wave.

Regardless, maybe it was just grief over Gram that had gotten Gramps bitter, but it was there.

"You can have your opinion if you want, but I've heard the church in Raspberry Ridge is quite good. They just got a new pastor, and he's pretty enthusiastic." Birdie pushed her chicken around again, looking back down at her plate after she spoke.

It was almost as though she didn't want him to look into her eyes. Again, she felt familiar to him.

"I'd really like to go, but probably not tonight. We weren't really planning on it, and Gramps has some things he wanted to finish in the cottage," Wesley said. He actually did want to go and planned to on Sunday, but Wednesday night church seemed a little bit much.

"The cinnamon rolls are done," Gram announced as the buzzer on the stove went off.

"And I think it's perfect timing, since it looks like everybody's cleaned their plate, except for Birdie," Gramps said, seeming to be grateful for the change of subject. He probably was. Church was not on his list of things he was happy about currently.

Wesley figured he would get over it, although honestly, Wesley had had enough of his own problems that he hadn't been thinking about Gramps's issues. He probably hadn't been as good to his grandpa after Gram died as he could have been. He had his own grief to handle.

Gram pulled two pans of cinnamon rolls out of the oven. "One of these is for supper, and one of these is for you guys to take home. I wasn't going to send them home unless you gave me my pie pan back. We have a small amount of space and not a whole lot of pans to go around."

"I'll bring you every pan in our cottage if you keep sending goodies like blueberry pie and cinnamon rolls home."

"All right. It's a deal," Gram said easily.

She seemed just as friendly and talkative as Birdie was not. A lot of times, the talkative ones got the attention. Low-hanging fruit, so to speak. But since her only competition was a seventy-year-old grandmother, his eyes seemed to be drawn back to Birdie. Did he know her from somewhere?

They ate the cinnamon rolls with a little bit of vanilla ice cream, and it was the perfect summer dessert. He could have gotten full just on the cinnamon rolls. But as a professional athlete, he knew he couldn't eat junk and expect his body to perform at peak levels, so he limited himself to two helpings.

The pan was cool enough for him to hold in his hands as he and Gramps walked away from the cottage less than a half an hour later. They didn't want to stay and keep the ladies from going to church.

"That lady can cook," Gramps said, and that was a huge compliment coming from him, considering that he considered his late wife the best cook of all time.

"I can't argue with you there. I ate so much I feel like I'm gonna pop."

"Same here. I think I ate just as much as you did, and that's pretty unusual."

"I think you ate more."

"Do you think Birdie was her given name?"

Wesley shrugged. "You said it was unusual, and she just kind of brushed you off. But I was wondering if it was a nickname, or something else."

"You should ask about it."

"Yeah. Maybe I'll ask her tomorrow when we meet on the beach." They had made those plans as they went out the door, that he'd be on the beach at one if she wanted to meet with him. She was there when he got back from his swim, and he thought that maybe she did it on a regular basis in the afternoon, although he hadn't noticed.

Mostly he took the swims in the morning, but today he'd decided to take two. Not just in anticipation of the idea that he would probably be eating more than he normally did, but because he had been a little bit on edge about meeting people and worrying about whether he was going to be recognized or not. Not that it exactly mattered. Two ladies in a cottage were not going to be a problem, but if they decided that they wanted to sell pictures to the paparazzi... And there was always the chance that they would read the negative stories about him and have an opinion that would make being neighbors with them awkward.

The papers were usually wrong in what they said, but he didn't typically have a chance to correct it. They had a microphone, and he didn't. Not unless he wanted to interrupt one of his press conferences and refute them, which he had never done. Although it had been tempting at times.

Sometimes though, the things that the papers printed were accurate.

In the case of what he had done after his grandma died, they had been.

It wasn't that he was proud of it.

"Are you sure you don't want to go to church? We didn't really have anything planned, although you do have some work you said you wanted to finish up."

"You can go if you want to, kiddo. I'm not going to. Not today."

That was a step forward. He hadn't shut the door on ever going again, like he had back home in Virginia.

Wesley took heart, and as much as he wanted to go to church just to see Birdie again and see if he could recognize where he knew her from, he decided that his questions could wait until tomorrow or some other time. There was no point in pushing things. After all, once he knew who she was, she would know who he was, and he wasn't sure if he was ready for that.

B irdie walked out the door, calling to Gram that she would be back in two hours, then closing it softly behind her and walking off the porch.

She had thought about skipping out or showing up late, but she would feel bad not showing up after she said she would, and she just couldn't be late on purpose. The Holy Spirit in her would not allow her to treat someone that badly.

Not that she hadn't been late plenty of times because of things she couldn't control, but it was the idea of deliberately not caring about a person enough to show up on time.

She had a little energy today and didn't feel so heavy inside. She'd also eaten a little bit of the cinnamon rolls that had been left over from supper for breakfast. They had been delicious.

Gram had already made lunch and was working on supper. She had given instructions to Birdie that she was supposed to invite Wesley and Gramps to come.

She felt like maybe that might be a little much. Perhaps the men didn't want to spend every evening with them, but Gram had insisted, and Birdie wasn't going to tell her no. She stepped down the steps onto the sand and saw Wesley standing at the bottom of the steps that led from his cottage. She hadn't seen him from the top, although her eyes scanned the beach.

"Hey. I wasn't sure whether you were going to show up or not," he said, carrying a small laptop and coming toward her.

She clutched her notebook and pen. She always wrote songs better when she had a pen in her hand.

She had checked in with her business earlier that day on her laptop. There were so many things to keep track of and things she needed to run, and while she had a business manager and a group of other people who worked for her who were supposed to handle the day-to-day activities so she didn't have to, it was up to her to make sure that everything was going the way it was supposed to.

"I said I would," she said, walking toward him and thinking that those words did not even hint at the temptation she felt to just stay in the cottage. Maybe part of the reason that she came was because she knew it would just be a simple matter of him walking a few steps to their cottage to see what was going on with her. And since the cottage was all one room except the bathroom, she would have no choice but to be there when the door was opened. Unless she was going to hide out in the bathroom all day.

There were times where that idea didn't seem so terrible.

"A lot of people say they'll do things, and then they end up not. You just never know anymore," Wesley said, sounding like he knew what he was talking about.

She noted another tight T-shirt, this one a different color, a bluish gray, and the closely cropped hair.

He had a nose that looked like it had been broken and a scar on the bottom of his jaw that she'd noticed the day before at supper.

"Is there a certain spot where you'd like to sit?" he asked, and she figured that she might as well try to get her head in the game since she obviously wasn't getting out of this.

"No. Just I like to sit as close to the water as I can without actually getting wet."

"So you don't like to get wet?"

"I don't like to be wet and cold at the same time." She lifted her shoulder, knowing that it was a little bit weird, but it was the truth. And he'd asked.

"You mean even on a hot summer day, you don't like to get in the lake and be refreshed with a little dip?"

"I'll do it, and I love to swim, but... I'd like to swim in bathwater, if I could. That would be nice."

"That's gross," he said. "I grew up in upstate New York, and the water's cold year-round. It's the best water to swim in. You get in there, and you feel like a new person when you get out."

"I'll take your word for it."

"You mean this writing session doesn't include a swim? Even though we're right by Lake Michigan?"

"I'll hold your computer while you go," she suggested with a lopsided grin. She knew he was just teasing her, and she appreciated him breaking the ice a little. She hadn't been sure that she was actually going to like working with him. And she really hadn't been sure whether she was going to be able to write a song, let alone multiple songs, while he was around.

"All right, how about here?" he asked, just shy of where the pebbly sand started to get wet. It was a perfect spot.

"This is good," she said, impressed that he had actually listened to her and had chosen a spot that he knew that she would like. That was... considerate. And despite herself, she was a little bit charmed.

"All right, I'll just admit this, I was thinking about it yesterday, and I could tell that there were some things at dinner that you were hiding."

"Wow, okay, let's jump in the deep end right away."

"Well, I was going to ask you how things went at church, but I didn't want to remind you that I hadn't gone, in case you were upset about that."

"Why would I be upset? It's your choice. That's between you and the Lord. If you want to get to heaven and explain to Him why you skipped out yesterday, go right ahead."

"He's not going to do anything."

"If you say so," she said, lifting a shoulder, but not looking at him, rather looking out on the lake, admiring the beauty in front of her. She didn't really think that God expected them to go to church every time the doors were open, except…it was good for them. She could tell a difference between when she was able to get to church on a regular basis and when she wasn't. Even the teaching last night had grounded her and challenged her in a way she felt was necessary.

"Wow. So you're legalistic about church attendance?" He looked down at his laptop. "All right then."

"Oh no. I told you, do what you want. God gives you free choice, why wouldn't I?"

"But you think I should have gone."

"No. I think *I* should have gone. And I did, and I'm glad I did. What you do is up to you."

He nodded and didn't say anything more.

"All right, let's jump back into the deep end."

"I think we've already been swimming there for a while. Pretty much every conversation I have with you is in the deep end."

She laughed, it was true, they started out talking about religion, which was supposed to be a taboo subject. "I suppose the next thing is that you're going to want to talk about politics?"

"No way. Not touching that, not for anything."

She laughed. "All right. You're right. There are some things I was trying to hide yesterday, and some things that I definitely don't want to talk about."

"Same." He said that immediately, which surprised her. And then he had a suggestion which she thought was really good. "What do you say we don't try to uncover each other's secrets. I was thinking last night I was kind of curious about what you weren't saying, but then I thought about how there were things I didn't want to say, and I figured you probably felt the same way about your secrets. So how about we just let the secrets stay buried, and we'll focus on other things. Deal?"

"Deal."

"You can tell me if I'm getting too close to something that is important to you."

"All right. I'll just tell you. I don't want to talk about who I am. Just Birdie, and that's enough."

"All right. I'm Wes, and that's enough."

They looked at each other for a moment, both of them with their eyes a little narrow, like this new piece of information—the fact that neither of them wanted their identities to be divulged—was interesting, and then they grinned at each other. Because they realized they were doing the very things that they had said that they weren't going to do, which was trying to figure out each other's secrets.

"This is a little tricky for me, because what I'm actually writing is an autobiography."

"Oh. Interesting." So he was famous enough that people might want to read his autobiography. She had been approached by several different places asking for her to write one, but she knew she didn't have the time. They had said that they could have a ghostwriter do it, but she wasn't comfortable with that. So, she was keeping notes about her life and thought perhaps one day... Perhaps.

"Yeah, which is going to be a little tricky because I was hoping you would help me with it. I... I'm not a writer in real life."

She laughed. "I'm not a writer either."

"But you've been carrying around the notebook and a pen."

"True. I do do a little bit of poetry like I said, but it's not my actual job."

"That stinks, because I have to have the first chapter of my autobiography written by Saturday. That's when... That's when it's supposed to go live."

"You're not publishing it in book form?"

"No. My... *Someone* suggested that I should start it out as a serial on social media." He seemed to be choosing his words very carefully so that he didn't give anything away. She could respect that, because she had the same care with her words.

"You must have quite a social media following if that's going to be profitable."

He blinked at her, and she thought maybe she'd said too much. Obviously she was a little bit knowledgeable about social media. But that shouldn't give away her actual identity or what she did for a living.

"I do. And maybe the book will increase that."

"I see."

"Anyway, I wasn't sure where to start. I guess that's what I was hoping for help with. That and... I don't know how to make the story compelling. I want to say this happened, and then this happened, and then that happened. But that doesn't seem very fun."

She thought about that for a bit. With her experience in songwriting, she knew that songs often told a story. And humans were hardwired to hear stories. They wanted to know what happened. Men and women were a little bit different. Where men had a tendency to want action, women wanted to know what the people in the story were thinking, but they all wanted a beginning, a middle, and an end.

But sometimes the structure could be twisted a little so that there was a hook right at the beginning. Like a song that started with a really catchy chorus, in order to grab people's attention and their ear, kind of get their foot tapping and their minds flowing along with the music before the story started. And then, the story would be interrupted every once in a while with that same attention-catching, toe-tapping, mind-grabbing chorus.

It didn't have to be that way, but it could.

"Is there an exciting event in your life that everyone is curious about? Something that people might not know the ending to, that you could grab them with right away? A hook, if we're going to use a fishing analogy. You want to bait the hook, cast it, and grab them right away with that."

"I suppose," he said thoughtfully.

"Or is there something that people don't know, something in your childhood that you could start with that would leave people curious? People who know you might think, 'wow, how did he get out of that,' and people who don't know you might think, 'how did he get into it?' You know?"

"I see. Something exciting that you're gonna stop in the middle."

"Yeah. Which you'll finish later after people are invested. It's like saying, did you hear that the dam broke?"

"And then, once you grab their attention with the fact that the dam broke, then you can go back to the beginning and start talking about how there had been a lot of rain in the area and the government had diverted funds to teaching diversity instead of taking care of the infrastructure of the country and... There you go. We just started talking about politics," he said, shaking his finger at her and teasing.

"You're right. I did. I just shook my finger at you, didn't I?"

"I'll pretend I didn't see it."

"But it's going to affect how you play."

"True."

He didn't even bother to deny it, and there wasn't anything she could do to get it back.

She tried hard to keep politics out of everything that she did, not that she didn't have opinions, but she had fans on both sides of the aisle, and she wanted to keep it that way. Plus, she wanted to have less influence about politics and more influence about religion. She hadn't been shy about talking about that.

"All right, I think I know where I can start. But this isn't just about me. You said you had writer's block too. Do you really have to write?"

"I actually do, but it's just a small part of what I do."

She hoped that he would think that she was an advertising exec, or something along those lines, where she had to write a catchy little jingle.

"What are you writing about? Can you give me a hint so I can help you?"

"I have some leeway in what I can write, but right now, I'm thinking about peace. That was the only word I got written down yesterday when I was sitting here."

"Seriously? You sat here the whole time I was swimming, and you only wrote one word?"

"How many words do you have written?" she asked, knowing that he had said that he didn't have any.

"None."

"And how long have you been trying to write?"

"All right. You got me. Six months."

"Six months, and you have zero words." She shook her head. "At least, if I've been trying to write for six months, I have one word. I win."

"You have one hundred percent more than I do."

"I think your math might be a little bit off," she said. "I hope you're not an accountant in your real life."

"Maybe I work on the space shuttle. Maybe that's why they're having so much trouble with everything. They got someone in there who isn't good with numbers."

"All right. I can see why you're trying to become an author. Because that space shuttle job is not gonna work out for you."

They laughed a little together, and she lifted her face to the breeze, allowing it to push her hair behind her, what was left of it after she chopped it all off. She had to admit that she missed it. Kicking her shoes off, she dug her toes into the rough sand and smiled, not thinking about anything in particular.

"Peace is being alone, or is it being with someone? And not feeling like you have to talk all the time?"

His voice came while she had her eyes closed, and she opened them, looking at him. "I often wonder that."

"I can help you a little better if you could give me an idea of what you're looking for."

"No, no. That was perfect," she said, flipping her pen in her hand and jotting a few words down. "This is four times as much as I did yesterday," she said, grinning.

"Is peace a theme? Are you thinking about things that give you peace? Because just seeing your toes in the sand, and feeling the lake breeze, made me feel peaceful. Although, having the water flow over me, and being underwater with the muffled sounds, and the fuzzy vision if I even bother to open my eyes, while everything flows over my skin feels peaceful to me as well. I almost hate to come up for air."

She narrowed her eyes and looked at him, thinking about how peaceful it was to be under the water. She'd never really considered it. Even the waves were calm when she was below the water.

"You can roll over and just have your nose and mouth out."

"Yeah. Take a breath, and submerge back under. You don't even need to flip over. Just let the water roll over you."

"As long as it doesn't roll up your nose."

"You breathe out a little bit. It doesn't come up if there's pressure for it not to."

"There must be a trick I don't know," she said thoughtfully.

They lapsed into silence as he opened his laptop and started typing. She stared at the line that she jotted down, *beneath the waves, a silent song.*

She manipulated the words a little, adding to them and finally coming up with another phrase, *cool touch of water's grace.*

She liked the ring to that one, and before long, she was immersed in her work and didn't notice the time flying by.

She was startled when he snapped his laptop closed. "I can't thank you enough. You jogged my memory, gave me some ideas, and I'm pretty happy with the way I started out. I can't say that this is exactly what I'm going to...put up on social media, but it's a great start."

She was opening her mouth to say that he also helped her, when thunder rumbled in the distance, and she looked up to see lightning flashing on the lake.

"Oh goodness, it's going to storm, and I hadn't even noticed." She realized that the breeze had gotten gusty, and clouds had rolled in overhead.

"Looks like it's going to be a doozy. Come on. I don't think we want to get caught out here when the lightning rolls in."

"No. That would probably be dangerous." She'd never actually been in a storm on the lake before, and she was kind of curious. Excited even. She always loved storms.

"You don't seem very scared," he said as they stood up and started walking toward the steps.

"I love storms, but I don't like to be wet. So I definitely want to get inside."

"I thought it was wet and cold."

"It's going to be cold. Can you feel the temperature dropping?"

He tilted his head and then nodded. "I believe you're right."

"Thank you," she said. "I got more done today than I've gotten for a while. I appreciate your perspective of how you feel underwater. I guess it's never hit me quite the same way, and you gave me some ideas."

"I think it's good when people who come from different backgrounds get together. Because you don't know what you don't know until you know it."

She laughed. "That's a great quote. You should put that in the book."

"I'll do that. And I'll add it was by your request."

Her face froze for a moment before she remembered that he didn't know who she was, and he was just teasing.

"You do that. I'll sign your book for you."

"It's going on social media, remember? There's nothing for you to sign."

"See you later," she said, laughing and throwing up a hand, and hurried off as he did, going to their respective steps.

She couldn't believe what a good time she had. She hadn't expected it, hadn't expected to like him so much, and hadn't expected for them to come to a compromise. For him to be so open about him hiding things and noticing that she was hiding things too, and for them to agree to just leave well enough alone. It took all the stress out of the conversations and their interactions, enabling her to relax and enjoy it.

To relax and write.

"Oh goodness, I think it's really going to storm," she said as she opened the screen door and slipped in, careful to close it softly behind her.

"You always liked them," Gram said from where she worked next to the stove. She hadn't even realized that it was almost time for supper.

"That smells heavenly," she said. And her stomach growled. Which made her smile even bigger.

"You had a good time. Look at that smile," her gram teased.

"My stomach's growling!" she said, her eyes shining. She didn't deny that she had a good time, because she absolutely had, and it was a pretty big deal that she was hungry too, so there was that.

"Let me put this down, and I'll give you a hand with supper."

"You might want to brush your hair. I can handle this."

She put a hand on her head and realized that her short hair had blown all over the place. It made sense that short hair would be easier to care for than long hair, but she felt that wasn't always true. Of course, if one wanted to curl or straighten their long hair, then they could really get into a lot of time, but a natural look was easier to pull off on long hair than short hair, which was something she found out the hard way.

This was the first time in her life that she had hair that short. She didn't care for it and couldn't wait until she could grow it out again.

She appreciated her gram noticing and sending her to brush it. For some reason, she wanted to look her best when Wes came over in just a bit.

Seven

"You're taking your tools?" Wes said as they prepared to walk out the door for supper.

"Figured I would. If they don't want me messing around in their house after supper, I'll just carry them back over. It's not a big deal," Gramps said as he carried his toolbox to the door.

"Let me carry it," Wes said. "I didn't do my workout today, and this'll catch me up a little bit."

He figured he needed to add that in order for Gramps to allow him to carry the tools.

"How do you think I stay so spry? It's because I carry my own tools."

"Why don't you carry the box of screws yourself then, and that'll take a little bit of weight out. Plus, I think it might fall out anyway."

"All right. That sounds like a deal," Gramps said, grabbing the box of screws, which probably did weigh close to five pounds. His toolbox was not a small one.

Wesley had to stop himself from whistling as they walked out of the house. He'd been smiling at the oddest times for the last fifteen minutes, even though the storm kept coming closer, and it felt like the lightning was striking just off the shore in the lake.

He wasn't overly fond of storms, not that he was afraid of them, just...preferred to have weather that wasn't storming. He'd been locked outside during a thunderstorm once when he was a kid and hadn't liked them since.

Still, he was looking forward to seeing Birdie again. It wasn't even that they had such an enlightening conversation. It had just been gentle teasing, and she'd prompted his brain in such a way that it had unleashed a whole torrent of words. He felt like he'd set a really good hook, and he was actually eager to dive into his story, but not so eager that he would skip supper.

He hoped to have helped her just as much, and he thought maybe he had, because she spent the entire time writing. If she'd only gotten one word written the day before, then she'd gotten a ton more work done with him. Hopefully that gave him a few brownie points, since he was planning on asking her if she wanted to do it again.

He followed Gramps up their stairs and then waited while Gramps rapped on the screen door. The storm door was open, almost as though they were anticipating the storm and enjoying the breeze.

"I hope you don't mind if your napkin is underneath your plate today. They kept blowing off the table," Gram said as she opened the door for them to come in.

"Our only concern is about the food, napkins are secondary," Gramps said, walking in holding the box of screws.

"My goodness, what do you have there?" Gram said, looking at the toolbox that Wes carried.

"The young whippersnapper thinks he's a big shot and wanted to carry my toolbox. Relegated me to this box of screws," he said, holding up the screws as evidence.

"What in the world are you bringing your toolbox over here for?" Gram asked, sounding perplexed.

It was like they hadn't talked about exchanging food for work yesterday, or maybe she thought they were joking.

"You have some windowsills that need to be fixed, don't you?"

"But I don't have any wood," she said.

"I was going to send the youngster back over to the house for some of ours. He'll have to cut it and bring it back. I didn't bring my saws over."

"Oh, nice," Gram said. "Go ahead and set the stuff down, and you guys can wash up for supper. Birdie is in the bathroom preening."

"I'm not preening," Birdie said as she opened the door at the back of the cabin and stepped out of the bathroom. Her hair had been straightened from where the wind had messed it up earlier. He liked the mussed look a little better, but he would never tell her that. She looked more natural, happier somehow. In a way that stirred his soul. "Gram told me to comb my hair because it was all messed up from the wind."

"That was ten minutes ago," Gram said to Gramps with a wink.

"Well, there were some other things I had to take care of while I was in there. Do I need to go into details?" Birdie said with a teasing glint in her eye. She seemed a lot lighter, a lot looser, more relaxed than she had the day before. Was that because of spending the afternoon with him? Or was she just happy that she'd finally gotten some of her writing done? Whatever her job was, whether it was a marketing exec or something where she had to come up with short little catchy slogans for advertisements, or something else, he was glad that she seemed to be able to work.

"No, child. You can spare us those details. I think you know better," Gram said, her words sounding more serious than her tone. He liked the teasing between the two of them. It reminded him of him and Gramps. There was definitely a respect there on his end, but it wasn't a fearful respect, it was an affectionate love, and a confidence that no matter what he did, his gramps was going to be okay with it. Even to the point of getting suspended from his job.

He had to admit he had a little bit of trouble taking his eyes off Birdie; she just seemed to glow. But he followed Gramps to the sink and started washing his hands as a crack of thunder exploded overhead. A gust of wind blew at the same time, and the screen door flew off its hinges.

"Goodness, I wasn't expecting that," Gram said as she hurried to grab the screen door. Birdie followed her out, and they leaned it against the railing, with one of the rocking chairs that sat on the porch pressed against it to keep it stabilized against the railing so it wouldn't blow away.

They came in, closing the door behind them. Two seconds later, the dark clouds opened, and rain poured down. Wesley knew this because almost as soon as the rain started coming down, it started leaking in the window over the sink where he stood.

A gust of wind blew it so hard that a drop landed on his nose.

"All right, I guess we were one storm too late in fixing this window. It's leaking."

He remembered what Birdie had said about not liking to be cold and wet.

"I think we should start with this window, Gramps," he said.

"I'm thinking we should start with the roof," Gramps said as he watched drops of rain hitting one of the plates on the table.

"The roof leaks?" Birdie said incredulously, like she couldn't imagine such a thing happening. Maybe she couldn't. It was probably the stuff of nightmares if she hated to be cold and wet as much as she had said.

Just then, a big crack of lightning snapped what felt like right beside them, cutting between the two cottages, and thunder roared immediately following it.

"That was close," Gram said as the thunder rumbled away.

She had no sooner said that than the lights snapped off.

They all stood there as though frozen, and Wesley tried to figure out what to say. It wasn't like they could fix it.

"Well, at least dinner is completely cooked."

"I can get some candles," Birdie said, going over to what must have been her side of the cottage and rummaging through one of the drawers of the dresser. Interesting that they weren't brimming with clothes. Most of the women Wesley had known had ten times as many clothes as he did.

Birdie seemed to dress pretty simply, but...he wondered if that was on purpose.

He kind of thought he might suspect who she was. At least, he had an idea.

Regardless, she came back with several candles.

"It's not dark now, but it will be, and we'll have the candlelight to make things cheerful for us while we eat."

"That's kind of you to consider the rest of us considering that you love storms." Gram's words were cheerful as she set a steaming casserole dish on the table.

"I never met anyone who really loved storms," Gramps muttered as he directed Wes to set his toolbox down just inside the door.

Water glasses had already been filled, and there was already a salad sitting on the table too.

"The only thing that's going to be messed up is the apple pie. It won't be cooked, since I had it timed to be ready to come out right after we were done eating."

"That's too bad, although I like apple pie well enough that I just might be okay eating it raw." Gramps settled himself into a chair.

"No. I will not allow you to eat it raw. That's just, ew."

They all laughed at Gram's exaggerated shudder and exclamation.

Before they started passing anything, Gram looked at him and said, "Would you like to say grace tonight?"

It didn't completely surprise him, since she had asked Gramps to say it the night before.

"Sure," he said, tempted to add that his grace would not be nearly as entertaining as Gramps's, but he didn't.

"Let's pray." He bowed his head and waited a second for everyone else to follow suit. "Lord God, thank you for the reminder of Your power and majesty in the storm that's raging outside. Thank you for the warm cabin and the relative dryness of it as well. Thank you for this food, thank you for the ladies who prepared it. Please bless it, amen."

He had to say relative dryness, since during the prayer he could hear the plunking of the water coming down from the roof and hitting someone's plate. His plate.

"I guess I'll just dump this water out," he said, grabbing his plate and carrying it carefully to the sink. The ladies twittered behind him, amused that the roof was leaking directly over his place setting.

He supposed he really didn't care. He didn't mind being wet, and he certainly didn't mind being cold. He'd grown up loving hockey, and he couldn't exactly play hockey without ice, so being cold was right up his alley.

If they had known that he was a hockey player, he might have made a joke about his preference that water be in its solid state. But he didn't want to make anyone question what was going on. No, that wasn't true, he didn't want to make *Birdie* question what was going on.

He sat back down in time to give his plate to Gramps who was dishing out casserole. Everyone else had a little bit of salad on their plates, so he grabbed some too. Salad wasn't exactly his favorite, but he knew that, again, he needed to fuel his body the best he could. Even though it was the off-season. He was working with a handicap, since he was going to be coming into the season late, and he supposed he should do everything in his power to make that handicap as slight as possible.

"So I guess it's good that we know where the cottage leaks now anyway," Gram said as they ate together, the rain still pounding on the roof. That sound, along with the flickering candles, somehow gave the whole cabin a cozy feeling to it.

"Do you really think that you'll be able to fix the window? And should we just get someone to fix the roof?"

"I can fix the window easily, and if Wesley is up to it, we can fix the roof. We used to do roofing way back, when he was a teen. He always gave me a hand and was quite good at it. But that might be beyond his pay grade now."

"I can put a roof on. The metal roof won't be hard at all. I'll need someone to help me though." He couldn't do it by himself, and Gramps wasn't going to be able to lift the pieces of metal onto the roof. "Actually, it would probably be helpful to have two people."

"I'm one," Gramps said.

"All right," he said slowly, trying to figure out how he was going to tell Gramps that he really didn't want him on the roof, and he also didn't want him handing the metal pieces up. They were sharp, and if he dropped one, it could kill him. But it wasn't like he had to reach up to a second story. The whole cottage was just one story. It would probably be okay.

"Maybe you can find someone in church on Sunday," Gram suggested.

"Maybe. I'll keep an eye out. Maybe there's something that I can do for someone else, and we can trade off." It wasn't like he had a whole ton of things to do. He just needed to write a book. And he got a chapter written today, so if he could write one chapter a day, even one chapter every other day, he'd have it done before his suspension was over.

And that was really all he needed.

"We'll have to have a few days to get the materials though. So you're going to have to deal with the leakage until then. Although we can get the window fixed as soon as the electricity comes back on."

"As long as it's not raining, we're not in any hurry," Gram said easily.

Wesley noticed that Birdie actually ate a few bites of her food today. Maybe she had just been nervous because of the company, although she didn't seem like the shy, retiring type that couldn't eat in front of people. He'd met girls like that, and they'd been a lot less competent than Birdie.

Regardless, he was happy to see her eating. Maybe being out with him for several hours had stirred up an appetite. Or maybe she'd eaten something before supper yesterday and hadn't been hungry.

He supposed it really wasn't any of his business, and if he really wanted to know, he should ask.

They finished the supper by candlelight, and as natural daylight faded and the lights did not come back on, he caught Gramps's eye. They should probably go.

Gramps seemed to agree, and it wasn't long before they took their leave.

The rain had long since quit, and the night was almost upon them. The whole world smelled fresh and clean, and the clouds had actually parted in the sky to show stars.

"That's a summer storm; here one second, gone the next," Gramps said as they walked down the steps and headed toward their cottage. They had left Gramps's toolbox with the ladies along with the box of screws, telling them they would be back in the morning to get the window fixed.

That was the way most storms were; they didn't last forever. Storms of life were the same, including his suspension and the grief of losing

Gram. Gramps hadn't said anything about her for the last two days, almost as though meeting Gram and Birdie and getting some good food had made him...not forget about her, but made the sting of her death not hurt quite so bad. Part of losing someone was being lonely without them. They always left a hole that could never be filled, but preferably, when something got taken away, it was always nice to try to put something else in its place.

Whether that was people or things.

"It was nice to have some good food two nights in a row, and they invited us back tomorrow. You think they're just inviting us because they feel bad for us?" He didn't want to wear out their welcome, but he had to admit he wanted to see Birdie as much as he could. They'd already agreed they'd meet on the beach at one.

"I think they probably enjoy our company just as much as we enjoy theirs. Gram definitely likes to cook for people. She reminds me of your grandma." His words were said a little softer, less gruff than Gramps usually was.

"Same. I mean, she's not the same at all, but I agree with you, she reminds me of her. It feels good to be there. Cozy, like we're a family almost."

"You know, that Birdie is a nice girl," Gramps began.

Wesley put up his hands. "No. Don't even start. I'm already in enough hot water, trying to dig myself out of the hole I fell in after Gram passed. I don't want to get entangled with anyone."

Although he already had.

"You're meeting her tomorrow, and you seemed to enjoy her company tonight."

"I can be friends with her. That's fine. You were just talking families and all that good stuff, and I don't know where my future is right now."

"You don't need to play another day of hockey in your life. In fact, I believe I told you several times that I thought it would be a good idea for you to retire."

"I can't retire with this over my head. I need to, if not retire on top, at least retire with a clean slate."

"I can't argue with you there, son. That's probably wise."

"Thank you. You don't usually use that word in conjunction with me, so I'll take it."

"I don't mean to not use it. You do have a good head on your shoulders. Just sometimes you get a little hot."

Wesley didn't say anything. He hadn't really been hot when he'd gotten suspended. He'd just...been playing with so much concentration and determination that he hadn't looked to the right or to the left, just focused and intent on nothing but the puck. He hadn't really meant to hurt Jack Flipps, but the play had been out of his control, and he had been out of control as well.

Once he'd gotten out of the zone in his mind and realized what he'd done, it was too late and a huge brawl had started. He didn't even fight the suspension. He deserved it. He had let his team down, his coach down, his fans down, and his family down. Most of all Gramps.

If Gram had been alive, she would have been the first person to tell him that he'd done wrong, but she would have also been the first person to understand what had happened. He was just playing on autopilot.

He couldn't play with his emotions, because the grief was too deep.

Grandma and Gramps had been the only parents he knew, and losing Gram had been hard. Harder than he expected.

It also brought him face-to-face with his own mortality. That was cliché, but true. He wasn't going to live forever, and it had been an eye-opening realization, even though he had known it on a surface level all of his life. Just, a guy got to a certain age and realized that he was getting older, and old age wasn't that far away.

It had just been a lot, and since it was the last game of the season, the rules of their league said the penalty had to be assessed on the first games of the next season. He was lucky that the Icebreakers hadn't traded him.

But they were a decent team, family oriented, and he had played there for a long time. Plus, his contributions were apparently greater than a month's suspension.

Regardless, he was curious about Birdie, liked her, but only wanted to be friends. And Gramps had better get anything else out of his mind.

Eight

"You look just fine. And Wesley is going to like you no matter how you look," Gram said as she stuck her head in the bathroom where Birdie fussed with her hair.

"Gram. It's not about Wesley. I just don't want anyone to recognize me. Wednesday night, it was kind of dim and dark, but it's going to be broad daylight today, and I'd prefer to keep the town in the dark about my identity. If I want to have peace and quiet this summer, I've got to." That was mostly the truth, although Gram was pretty much right. She did want Wesley to see her, and like what he saw.

She glared at her stupid short hair. What had possessed her to cut it?

It was a rhetorical question, because she knew the answer and knew she had had a choice. She fussed with it just a little bit more and then grabbed the hairspray and closed her eyes, putting a cloud of vapor around her head.

It was going to have to do. Hopefully she fixed it in such a way that her identity was safely hidden. Plus, she had a rather large pair of glasses that she was going to wear as well. They had regular lenses in them and were totally for show or, rather, camouflage.

She had a couple of ideas about what Wesley's identity might be. She knew that he was a well-known figure as well. Maybe that's why he was so considerate about her and her preference to not have her identity known. Who better to understand than someone who was going through it themselves, right?

There was an actor who looked very similar to him, but she'd been trying for several days to think of his name and couldn't.

But as they got in their rented Ferrari, and she backed out of the drive, she tried to put thoughts of Wesley out of her mind and instead focus on her gram.

"Gram, you know how when we go to church, and you have a tendency to sign up for everything?"

"Not everything," she said. "I never signed up to play the piano."

"That's because you can't," Birdie said, holding on to her patience admirably, if she did say so herself. "You have a tendency to sign up for everything but playing the piano," she started again.

"I want to serve the Lord. I want to do everything I can to help out, and I enjoy it."

"But we're not going to be here for very long, and you're already busy, and I'm supposed to be here to rest, not to run here and there and everywhere for church."

"I'm not signing you up, I'm signing me up." Her gram looked across the seat at her. "But if you want me to sign you up, I can."

"No!"

"Birdie. I raised you to be a servant. Just because you're a big, international—"

"I can be a servant." She took a breath. "You can sign me up for one thing, if you promise to limit yourself to two things."

"What about five things? You know how small churches are. They always have more jobs than they have people to fill them. And then they end up just throwing those jobs by the wayside because nobody wants to do them."

"Maybe they won't have a sign-up sheet for any jobs, and then you won't feel the need to sign up for anything."

"All you have to do is ask the pastor if he has any jobs for someone who's going to be around for a couple of months, and he can pull jobs out of his back pocket like you would not believe."

Birdie felt her forehead thumping. "Gram. Please."

"I know you're trying to rest, Birdie, and I'm here to help you. I promise that I will not miss cooking any meals for you, not even one. So I will not sign up for anything that will take me away from cooking breakfast, lunch, and supper, or at least having them ready for you to eat."

"Gram," she said wearily. Knowing she was fighting a lost cause. Serving made her gram happy. And she understood that. It made her happy to do things for other people too. To watch them smile, to know that she was a part of it, but they weren't going to be here that long. And she didn't want the church to depend on them, first of all, and secondly, she wanted to be able to take it easy.

"We can rest in heaven. The Bible says work for the night is coming."

"Isn't that a hymn?" Birdie said, wrinkling up her nose.

"I'm pretty sure it's a hymn *and* Bible verse. But you can look it up if you're not sure."

Birdie let it go. Her gram could quote circles around her from the Bible and the hymnbook.

She enjoyed driving the Ferrari. She'd never driven anything quite so nice. It purred under her hands and was so responsive she almost overcorrected as she got out on the main street of town. It was just a short trip up the street to the church, and she felt like she hadn't driven it nearly enough. Maybe she could take a ride later.

"Just, Gram. Please, give us a week or two to settle in before you start volunteering for everything."

"I told you. I'm not going to volunteer for everything." Her gram nodded her head. And then she sighed, looking over at Birdie with an expression that Birdie could hardly deny. "I'm just used to being busy. I need to be busy. And there's no water aerobics here, no spinning classes, no Rotary club, no bridge with my friends, no community walks, no volunteering at the local Salvation Army, no doing my Meals on Wheels, and that's just the stuff I do on Mondays."

"I know, Gram. It's a small town."

"I know. I just want to be a blessing."

"All right. You be a blessing." Maybe she'd have to rent a house that was separate from her gram. But she knew she never would. Her gram wasn't going to invite people over to the house. She was just going to be busy going to and fro, doing as much as she could.

She pulled into a spot in the church after waiting for a family to walk across the parking lot, and she cut the motor. She and Gram got out, and she smiled again at the car. She didn't think she'd want to own one, but it was fun to drive one for a little bit.

"I love church, I love it," Gram said, taking a hold of her elbow as she waited for her at the back of the car.

"I know you do. And I love it too." She really did. She loved the singing, she loved being with other Christians, in a room full of people who believed the way she did. How often did that happen around the world? Never. She loved listening to the preaching, of seeing things in her life that she needed to work on, of being reminded that she needed to be close to Jesus, of being able to give and volunteer and just all the things that church represented, the things that she loved, and when she was on tour, they were all things that she couldn't have.

"Oh, look, there's Wes and Gramps," Gram said, pointing to the back of the church where Wesley and his grandfather stood chatting with two men Birdie didn't know.

She looked around, wondering if her good friend Olive had arrived. She hadn't tried to call Olive, although she texted her and let her know that she arrived safely. Olive had just gotten married, and Birdie didn't want to interrupt a honeymoon, if they took one. She hadn't even asked.

"Wesley! Gramps! They came after all," Gram said in a stage whisper to her as she hurried across the parking lot, deliberately missing the open doors and heading toward the two men.

Wesley looked up. A big smile spread across his face.

Gramps saw them at the same time and said something more to the men they were talking to before they started to walk toward Birdie and her gram.

They met on the walk beside the church, with Gram practically hugging Gramps. "I didn't think you'd be here!"

"I could hardly not come, since the lady who cooks my food said I should."

"You silly man," Gram said, giving his arm a light tap and batting her eyes at him. Birdie tried to close her mouth. Her grandma never acted like that.

"Now, you have to make sure that you sign up for everything they offer you. If you say no one time, they might not ask again." She had grabbed a hold of Gramps's arm and started steering him toward the church. She looked over her shoulder, calling, "Wesley, dear. I'll go ahead and sign you up for something. Birdie told me I could sign her up for one thing, and I assume you probably feel the same. Although, if you want more, I'm certainly happy to oblige."

Wesley jerked his head without saying anything, because Gram had already hurried Gramps out of the way, and Birdie assumed he wasn't sure his voice would carry that far.

"I'm sorry about that."

"Has she ever even gone to this church before?"

"Just Wednesday evening."

"Wow. She could recruit people to wear bikinis in Antarctica, and I think they'd probably get some."

"Yeah. By forcing them on them," Birdie said, trying not to sound bitter. Her grandma had just railroaded Wesley into doing something that he might not have wanted to, and he didn't even know what it was. "I'm sorry about that. I hope she doesn't sign you up for anything terrible."

"I'm a big believer in giving back to the community. I don't mind doing something."

"She might have you digging up the septic system. I actually did that once at our church. No one would sign up for it, so Gram signed me up."

"Interesting."

"Actually, it was good for me. I was in Africa on, well, just because, and they were having some trouble with their septic. I had experience in running a shovel anyway."

"Nice. So you never know when the stuff that your gram gets you into is going to pay off? Is that the moral to the story?"

"I guess we're trying to look on the bright side, right?"

"That's always a good idea."

"I can't say I disagree with you, but... I warned you."

"Noted," he said as he turned and started slowly strolling beside her toward the church.

A family, with what looked like twin babies and four half-wild children, hurried into the church ahead of them.

"Six kids. Wow."

"Yeah, that's crazy."

"You're one of those millennials who don't want children?"

"I guess I never really thought about it. I suppose it would depend on who the dad was. I don't want to do that by myself for sure. But it looks like she has help."

They had developed an easy camaraderie over the last three days from meeting every afternoon for a few hours. She had worked a little more on a couple of songs, but the song that was focused on peace and the feeling of being in the water and sand was her favorite.

She helped Wesley get a few more chapters in, and he seemed confident that he would be finishing the book well before he needed to. She had asked if he was going to let her know when the first chapter dropped, but he had just smiled at her, and she had remembered their agreement. Of course he couldn't tell her when it dropped, or at least he couldn't point her to it so she could read it, because then she would find out his identity.

"You know Gram invited us over for dinner after church, right?" Wesley said as they stepped inside the auditorium.

"I do. She had something in the crockpot, and it smelled delicious. I'm looking forward to it."

"Can I ask you something?" He stopped when they reached the back of the sanctuary, and leaned down.

"Sure."

"Do you mind us coming over so much?" He looked around, and then he said, "We've been there every day."

"No. In fact, it's kinda cozy. I don't mind it, and I know Gram loves it."

"All right. You'd tell me if there was a problem?"

"Probably," she said, being perfectly honest. Sometimes it was just easier to swallow irritation than it was to tell someone that they irritated you. Most of the time, it didn't really matter.

Wes gave her a long look, and then he said, "I'll see you in a little bit."

She nodded and had to keep herself from watching him walk away.

"Birdie?" A voice whispered in her ear, and then an arm went around her.

"Olive!" She wrapped her arms around her friend whom she hadn't seen in years and squeezed tight.

"Congratulations on your wedding!" she said, standing back to look at her friend who had changed a little, but not so much that she wouldn't have recognized her.

Olive looked both ways before she said, "I almost didn't recognize you. That's a really good disguise."

"I hope it's enough to keep everyone else from recognizing me. I'm trying to lie low. I can't do that if people are constantly trying to take pictures of me." She kept her voice down so no one overheard their conversation.

"Well, it doesn't help that I was just in Blueberry Beach this week, and there's a huge billboard announcing your new album, with a big picture of you on it."

"Oh no." She knew that the advertising blitz was going out for the album she had dropped earlier in the year. There were new songs releasing, and the marketing company she had hired was doing a countrywide blitz on those.

"I can't fix it now though." It was too late to cancel it. The money had already gone out.

Plus, that was part of how she made her living, making money on her singles on various digital media channels. She didn't exactly want to stop it. It would just be nice if they could have done that media blitz without her face. At least in Michigan.

"Well, it is what it is," she said.

"I'm sorry. I shouldn't have given you the bad news. I don't want to upset you or make you worry about it."

"No. I'm fine. I can't change it, and I do look a good bit different now." Her hair was shorter and a different color, plus she wore glasses. When she looked in the mirror, she felt like she was looking at a completely new person.

"So I assumed I didn't hear from you because you knew I had just gotten married, but we're back from our short honeymoon trip, and I'd really like to get together sometime. Are you free at all?"

"Any morning this week. Unless Gram signs me up for something here at the church, which she's been known to do."

"I remember you talking about her. She seems like quite the personality."

"She is," Birdie said with affection.

"She's not slowing down at all?"

"She's well into her seventies, but no. She's not slowing down at all. In fact, if anything, I think she's busier now than she used to be."

"Well, I guess that's a good thing. People are staying alive and active well into their seventies and eighties now."

"Yeah, it seems like when they hit eighty sometimes that's like a marker, but maybe not. I guess everyone ages differently."

"I think so. I've gotten to the point where I know I feel better if I exercise and eat right, I just can't always make myself do it." She rolled her eyes, and Birdie laughed, but she knew all too well how that was. With her job, she had to look good, since she was constantly in the public eye. It wasn't always easy. And it certainly wasn't pleasant.

"Oh. I better get going. My sister's waving to me. Good to see you," Olive said as she gave Birdie one more squeeze and then hurried away.

Birdie looked around for her gram and saw her talking to a group of people.

She wasn't sure where she had picked out a seat, or even if she had, so she slipped into a pew near the back that wasn't bursting at the seams. It seemed like everyone who could possibly live in Raspberry Ridge had come to hear the new pastor. Or maybe, he was just that good.

He was just that good, she decided to herself an hour later as the last hymn was sung and the pastor had dismissed the congregation. The sermon had been excellent, and the singing of the old hymns perfect. She remembered each one from childhood, and they all brought back good memories, as well as reminding her of what a good message they had.

She left with her heart full, and after shaking the pastor's hand and thanking him for the good sermon, she walked slowly out into the sunshine, chatting with some ladies along the way, knowing that it would probably be a while before Gram got out. Birdie always liked to wait for her outside, in the summer anyway. After spending so much time inside, it was nice to go out and get warm.

She enjoyed the sunshine on her face and the light breeze, bracing and sweet.

"You spend a lot of time with your eyes closed and your face lifted to the lake. Is that like a meditation thing?"

She laughed at the voice in her ear. "I think everyone who lives by the lake is supposed to strike a pose like that at least six times a day. Have you gotten your quota in yet?"

She turned to Wesley and grinned at him. He was easy to talk to, and fun. And while she felt an underlying attraction, she knew that her schedule was not for the faint of heart, and if he was famous in his own right, it was almost guaranteed that they wouldn't be compatible. Which was a shame, because she really did like him.

"So has anyone recognized you?" he asked, looking around and keeping his voice pitched low, which she appreciated.

"No," she said under her breath. "You?" She couldn't believe she was even asking.

"Not that I know of. Which is all well and good." He looked around, and then with narrowed eyes, he said to her, "What about you? Have you figured it out yet?"

She knew immediately that he was asking if she had figured out who he was. "I actually have some ideas, but I haven't thought about it too hard, because I don't think I want to know."

"Same and same," he said with one side of his mouth curling up into a smile.

The moments ticked by as they stared at each other, Birdie barely registering that other churchgoers were walking around her, chatting and laughing.

It just seemed like a perfect day. One with no worries and no pressure.

Nine

"So did you sign up for anything?" Wesley asked with the wicked glint in his eye that told her he remembered their conversation when she had told him that her gram had a tendency to sign up for everything.

"I'm sure Gram will take care of it. I told her just one thing though." Birdie's lips pulled back a bit, and she lifted her brows. "You?"

"I figured your grandma would take care of me too. So I didn't need to. Although I was asked if I would be interested in joining the men's sailing club."

"I didn't know there was a sailing club." She hadn't heard mention of that, and a quick glance at the list hanging on the bulletin board as she exited the church had not divulged any kind of sailing club.

"They're just starting it. They wanted to know if I would be the chairman."

"Really?" she asked, and then she tilted her head. "Do you know how to sail?"

He snorted. "I've never been on a boat in my life before."

They laughed together. That was so typical of churches. At least in her experience, if you weren't dead, they'd recruit you for something, and it didn't matter if you were good at it.

"Well, maybe that's what Gram will sign you up for. And you'll get an education this summer."

"I think I'll probably be the only chairperson of a sailing club that got their sailing education from the internet."

"Oh, I think we'd be surprised," she said, figuring that there were plenty of people in positions who didn't know what they were doing. And relied on the internet to teach them.

"At least we can cheat in our day and age," she said, although she wasn't sure that using the internet was cheating. It was basically taking someone else's expertise and learning from it. Although, reading about something was a lot different than actually doing it. Especially in the case of something like sailing.

"3D printers are going to have to start printing out lakes and boats if I'm going to be totally self-taught."

"I'm hungry," Gramps said as he joined them.

"I know lunch will be on the table just minutes after we get in the house, but sometimes getting Gram away from church is a little bit difficult. We're often the last people out of the parking lot."

"We should have invited them over to our house today," Gramps said as an aside to Wesley, who immediately shook his head quickly.

"We don't want to kill our neighbors. We like them, remember?"

"But I'm hungry!"

"We will get far better food, far faster, if we just relax and be patient. Neither one of us can cook worth anything."

"I wonder if Gram gives cooking lessons," Gramps said, looking around to see if he could try to find her.

"I'm sure she would love to give you cooking lessons. Maybe in exchange for fixing our windows and roof."

"Which, I'd forgotten to say, the materials should be arriving tomorrow. We can get that roof on if it's okay with you guys?"

"Any time is fine with us," Birdie said, and most of her thought that was true. There was one small part of her that was concerned that her grandma was going to sign them up for so many things that she wouldn't have a free moment from now until she left the beach cottage.

She didn't voice that thought out loud. There was no point in borrowing trouble. Perhaps Gram had gotten a little bit more restraint since last time they'd been in church together. Doubtful, but she was holding on to hope.

"Well, son. How about you and I go home and we can get our clothes changed. I think the ladies will be fine if we don't wear a suit and tie to Sunday dinner."

"This lady will be relieved if you don't dress up for dinner," Birdie said. "If you come in a suit and tie, I'm going to have to wear this dress, and I would prefer to change into something a little bit more comfortable."

Wesley snorted, and Gramps gave him a look.

Wesley held his hands up. "She looks good in whatever. I didn't say anything."

"We'll see you in a bit," Gramps said as Wesley lifted a hand to wave, still smiling, which she returned. Both the grin and the wave.

She looked around the churchyard and still didn't see her gram, but she saw a young girl standing off by herself, and something drew her toward her. There seemed to be something tragic about her stance, and she just seemed...sad, almost. Or maybe just very alone amongst a whole group of people. Sometimes a person could be standing and not saying anything, and feel like they were part of the group, but this girl just seemed like she was floating on the outer edge.

Birdie wasn't really looking for friends or anyone to talk to, but she found herself walking to the young woman, who must have been in her early or mid-twenties she figured as she got closer to her.

"It's such a beautiful day," she said by way of greeting. Hoping that the girl wasn't into pop music. She felt like her "disguise" had been effective, but she didn't want to get cocky.

At the same time, she couldn't not walk over to this girl and try to engage her in conversation.

"I can't imagine not living beside the lake," she said, pulling her gaze from the lake long enough to smile and hold her hand out. "I'm Becky. I don't recognize you, but I haven't been here very long."

"I'm Birdie, and this is my first Sunday here, so it's no wonder you don't recognize me."

"You do look a little familiar, but I am originally from Strawberry Sands, so maybe I met you down there."

Birdie didn't want to have the girl trying to figure out why she looked familiar, so she just lifted a shoulder as though agreeing that it was possible, when she had never been to Strawberry Sands and knew it wasn't.

"So are you a shop owner?" Birdie asked, taking a wild stab in the dark, just trying to make conversation and figure out if there was something that she could say or do that would take away the melancholy look from the girl.

"Not really. I'm renting the farm down the road a piece and am hoping to rent horses for tourists to ride on the beach."

"I love horses, but I've never really gotten to ride." It was one of the things that she had always hoped to do but just never had time for. Her career didn't exactly lend itself to long rides on horses. "I think riding a horse on the beach would be a lot of fun."

"That's what I'm counting on. People thinking it's fun and being willing to pay for it. It's hard to make a living at it, but if I do a little bit of something else on the side, I might be able to at least have the horses pay for their own feed and care."

"You sound like you're rather knowledgeable about this. Are horses something you grew up doing?"

"Not really. But I've done a lot with horses in the last five or ten years. I... This is my first time starting out on my own though."

Maybe that was her trouble. The weight of owning her own business felt heavy even though she had experience and had been doing it for years. Of course, now, she had plenty of people hired to help her, but she had to manage it, or she couldn't expect it to thrive. No one cared about her business the way she did. To everyone else, it was just a job.

"You have someone helping you?" she asked, her tone gentle.

"No. I'm in it myself. But that's kind of the way I like it. I—" She started to say something, and her voice broke off abruptly.

Birdie waited, just in case she was going to finish her thought or change it, but she just went silent.

"It makes it extra hard when you're alone. And there aren't a whole lot of tourists in Raspberry Ridge right now. But I heard some whispers about a restaurant." That was something that Olive had told her might be coming. "And the fact that the church is opening up, and people are getting married... It's definitely a growing town. And you can get in on the property values before they go up."

"I don't have quite enough to put in a down payment to buy the farm, and I feel like I might need that as capital to run my business until it takes off."

"I think that's smart. Renting is not ideal, but some people have it as their business model." She pushed a strand of hair back away from her face. "What are you thinking about doing on the side? You said the horses would pay for themselves and their feed. What about the rent for the property?"

"I've been writing some articles online. I'm making a little bit of money. But with AI, I'm afraid that little bit of money is probably going to dry up."

Birdie had been concerned about the same thing with her songwriting. She wrote all of her own songs, but it took her months, sometimes years, to get an album's worth of songs. AI could do it in a matter of seconds. And they weren't terrible. It stood to reason that the improvements that would come along in the next several months, maybe even a year, would possibly put songwriters out of business.

"The thing that AI can't do is it can't be human."

"It makes a pretty good imitation of it though," Becky said, tilting her head like there was nothing she could do about it.

"Do you have a backup plan?"

"I started to get my nursing degree. But I'd rather do horses than nursing, and I can't imagine being stuck in a hospital day in and day out, so... I quit after two years."

"So you think you might go back?"

"Maybe. I probably should do it before I'm so strapped that I don't have any choices and can't afford to. But that's just not where my heart is, you know?"

"You could go to school to be a vet?"

"That's six more years. I don't think I can stand it." She shuddered.

"Vet tech?"

"Yeah. I thought of that."

They were silent for a bit. As Birdie looked around, she noticed the parking lot had thinned out, but there was still no sign of Gram.

"So what are you in town for? Are you a store owner?" Becky asked, echoing her earlier question.

"I'm not. I'm just a tourist, enjoying the peaceful serenity for the summer. Before I have to go back to my real life, which is not nursing, thankfully."

"Nurses have a hard job. It must be exhausting, although veterinarians work hard too. I guess that's why we call work a job."

"Yeah. I think we all want to find jobs where we really don't have to put too much effort into it and get paid a lot."

"I don't think I'd be happy with something like that. I want to work hard. I love the idea of building something, but unfortunately, sometimes when you're building, you're not making money, and that's important too."

"I agree," Birdie said simply. There were a lot of times when she had first started singing that she didn't have money to eat. If it hadn't been for her gram, she might have had to quit and do something else. And then the stratospheric career that she'd been able to have wouldn't have been possible. She owed her gram an awful lot.

"When you open your stable, I'd love to be the first customer." She loved horses and always wanted to ride. Why not start by being Becky's first customer?

"Really?" Becky's eyes lit up, and she looked years younger.

"Yes."

"I have the horses now, but I need to get another saddle. Maybe next week?"

"I think you should take advantage of the summer weather. You probably won't have much business in the winter."

"I have Gypsy Vanner horses. They're great saddle horses, but they also will pull a wagon or sleigh. They're beautiful, too."

"Ah. That's smart." Although she just wasn't sure if there weren't that many tourists in the summer, would there be enough in the winter? But maybe Becky had it figured out, or maybe she would.

She found herself rooting for the girl. There was something about her that reminded her of her grandma. Like Becky was what her grandma would have been when her gram was that age. Feisty, determined, and not allowing anything to stand in her way. Of course, her gram was a lot more of a people person, and Becky seemed a little bit more standoffish, even saying that she wanted to do things herself.

After a couple of minutes of careful consideration, she said, "How about I give you my number. You can call me when they're ready." She hesitated for just a moment as Becky pulled up her phone. "I live in one of the cottages on the north side of town, right down by the lake. You're welcome to visit anytime. If you come around lunchtime, my grandma would love to feed you."

She paused as Becky looked up at her. "And that includes today. Show up anytime."

"All right. Thanks. Maybe I will," Becky said, and then Birdie rattled off a number while Becky programmed it into her phone.

"I love riding bareback, but if you haven't ridden a lot, it's probably not the best way to start, although my horses are very gentle. I'll let you know when I have a saddle."

"All right. And I'll look for you around mealtimes. They're typical times, and if you come between mealtimes, Gram almost always has some kind of dessert sitting around that she loves to feed visitors. I'm serious. You will make Gram's day if you show up and she gets to feed you."

"I'll keep that in mind," Becky said, sending a text and then tucking her phone back in her pocket.

Birdie pulled up her phone and said, "Got it." She typed Becky's name into the contact info before shoving her own phone back in her pocket.

"So are you hanging around waiting for someone?" Becky finally asked.

"I live with my gram. And she has a bit of an addiction to volunteering, especially at churches. Or maybe she just has a fear of having one second that isn't scheduled during her day. I'm not sure."

Becky laughed. "Someone who likes to be busy and productive?"

"Yeah. And she really does mean well. I'm not complaining at all, because she is an awesome gram, I don't know what I would have done without her, literally, but I've got a feeling she's probably signed me up for at least one volunteer position that I really don't want."

"At least you have someone who cares about you. That's something to be thankful for, right?"

"Right."

"Well, I suppose I'll walk on home. I try to take Sundays off and not work. So I was kind of hanging around the church, because once I go home and sit down, I'll look around and see all the things that I should be doing or that need to be done, and I will want to get up and start doing something, telling myself that it's not really work if I enjoy it, right?"

"Well, good for you for taking some time off. I think it's important. Although, I suspect that most people nowadays take more than one day a week off and are more about taking time off than they are about working."

"Not me," Becky said, and there was still a bit of a sadness around her mouth, almost as though she were pushing the memories that she didn't want to think about away and not allowing them to crowd into her mind.

It was hard to take control of a person's thoughts, to make them go the way they wanted them to go or the way they needed to go. There was something rather fun about being morose and gloomy, in a weird kind of way. If a person wasn't careful, they could end up spiraling down without even realizing it, just because they were enjoying their gloomy thoughts.

Birdie had done that more than once in her life, and it was hard to climb back out of that kind of pit.

"Birdie!" Gram called, erupting from the church doors and blinking in the bright sunlight. "I thought you might have gotten impatient and driven away," she said, laughing.

"No such luck, Gram. You're stuck with me," she said, a little bit of dread in her stomach. It had been a long time, and Gram would have had time to sign up for pretty much everything the church wanted her to do.

"I thought maybe you'd be out here talking to Gramps and that nice Wesley boy," Gram said, bounding down the steps and hurrying across the parking lot to where Birdie stood alongside. The car wasn't far away; it was one of three cars left in the lot. She assumed one car was for the pastor, and one car had either broken down and was parked there, or there was a person who was more zealous than her gram, which was kind of hard to imagine.

"They were going home to change their clothes. I figured since they live beside us, they won't have a problem figuring out when we get home."

"Well, what are we waiting on? Let's go."

Ten

"I think we're finally ready to start," Wesley said as Birdie met him outside their cottage.

The roofing material was supposed to be delivered on Monday, but it had been delayed until Thursday. Now, it was bright and early on Friday morning, and they were ready to get started. They had gotten Miles, whom Pastor Garnet had recommended, to give them a hand. Pastor Garnet had also come, which hopefully would negate the need for Gramps to do too much work.

"That's great. I was happy that we hadn't had any more rain this week. Or you might have had two extra visitors in your cottage."

"You know you're welcome anytime," he said, smiling down at Birdie and thinking about what a great time he had with her every afternoon this week. She'd shown up on the beach, he brought his writing and she brought hers, and they chatted back and forth, helping each other. He'd gotten three more chapters written, and he couldn't be happier.

His agent wanted an editor to go over them before they were released on social media, so he might have some editing to do, but at least the chapters were written.

He had Birdie to thank.

"As much as you've had Gramps and me over to eat, we owe you more than we could ever repay."

"Unless Gramps becomes a world-class cook and starts inviting us over there."

"Thanks for coming up with that idea," Wesley said immediately. As soon as he'd heard that the materials were going to be delivered on Thursday, he had asked Birdie to see if her grandma would give cooking lessons to Gramps on Friday. It turned out that Gram had volunteered to teach a cooking class for the folks at the church, and since she had been declared the chairperson, she decided that the first meeting of the newly christened group would be Friday morning. Gramps didn't want to miss it, so they were hoping that would keep him inside and not out trying to put a roof on.

"Not that he can't do it," Wesley said, and Birdie nodded.

"I get it. You just want to keep them safe at that age. Although, he gets around as well as anyone I've seen, except for Gram. No one can hold a candle to her."

"I'd like to argue with you on that, because I don't really like the idea that your family is winning, but... It's true. Your grandma is quite a lady."

"She sure is. Did I tell you everything she signed up for at church?"

"You told me that she signed you and me up to help take care of Vera and Dominic's twins and four other children."

That had been a shock. He hadn't really thought the old lady was actually going to sign a complete stranger up for anything. But she had. It almost made him chuckle, because she had signed Birdie and him up to be there together. Which he found interesting. Was the old lady matchmaking? Or was she afraid that he wasn't going to show and she wanted her granddaughter there for insurance that the job would actually get done?

He hadn't quite been able to ask Birdie her opinion on it yet, but he planned to at some point.

"It was just you and me, and she did keep us to one thing, which was kind of surprising,"

He laughed, knowing that Birdie probably wasn't exaggerating at all.

"So what did she sign up for? A couple other things? Besides the cooking class."

"She signed up for cooking class, to be a greeter, an usher, to mow the church lawn, which isn't hard since Vera and Dominic take care of the cemetery, but still."

"She signed up to mow the grass?" He shook his head. "Does the church even have grass?"

"She sure did. A little bit of grass, if you look around. It's mostly weeds. And she actually already did it. She bought a pair of scissors at the store expressly for that purpose and went to the church and used her scissors to cut the grass."

"You're kidding," he said, running a hand through his hair and shaking his head in disbelief. That lady was something else.

"No. But she did what she signed up for."

"Was that it?"

"No. She also signed up to visit the assisted living center, take meals to seven different shut-ins, do two ladies' grocery shopping, clean the sanctuary on the first Sunday of every month, and scrub toilets after every service."

"Is that all?"

"I might be forgetting a few things. She has it all written down. But the thing is, she'll do it all, she won't complain about it, she'll love it, and, oh! She also is leading the new handbell choir, as director and head handbell player."

"So she's a musician?"

"She doesn't read a note."

"Wow."

"I know, and she's donating the handbells, so the church is going to have handbells, and they're going to have a handbell choir, and Gram is going to lead it, and..."

"She should have been a general."

"I know, right?" She laughed, shaking her head. "No fear."

"I guess it's not Gramps that I need to worry about coming out and getting on the roof. Seems to me like it's your gram that we need to try to keep down."

"Well, the cooking class is pulling double duty with him

participating in it and her leading it. Hopefully it'll keep both of them safe."

"I should probably take some cooking classes, seriously. I can't cook a lick. And I didn't realize how terrible I was until I tried to do it myself. I have a—" He snapped his mouth shut.

They hadn't talked about their personal lives at all. But there had been this bond that had been growing between them, a bond where both of them knew that both of them were trying to keep their identities on the down-low, to not talk about their actual lives, because they were both famous.

He hadn't figured out exactly what Birdie was, but he had his suspicions.

She gave him a knowledgeable grin and then wagged her finger back and forth in front of his nose. "Oh. You almost did a boo-boo." She laughed and then turned back to the cottage, calling over her shoulder, "We'll be out with some water periodically."

"Thanks."

She was right. He had almost started to talk about his life, because he felt so safe with Birdie. She seemed like such a down-to-earth, regular person. She made him feel that way too. Because she wasn't always going on about his superstar status, or ogling his muscles, or acting like he hung the moon. That was the kind of treatment he was used to from most people, especially in his hometown where he was pretty well known.

But Raspberry Ridge was growing on him, and he definitely wouldn't mind staying here in the off-season. He wasn't even sure he would mind moving here. Especially if he had some incentive, like a beautiful neighbor who was also funny and sweet and helped him be a better version of himself and lived here year-round. He would definitely have to think about it at that point.

Sighing, he saw that Miles and Pastor Garnet had just pulled in, stopping between the cottages since there was no spot to park the pickup.

Miles brought a ladder, so he walked over to give them a hand carrying it over. He had thought about renting a scissor lift, but with how small the cottage was, they could handle it themselves. A scissor lift would be overkill. He really didn't even think it would take the entire day to put the metal pieces on. Once they got them started, they went really fast, and the pastor had said Miles was an experienced roofer,

"Wesley, you got a beautiful day to put a roof on," Pastor Garnet said as he came around the end of the truck.

"Somebody must have an in with the Being who controls the weather. He gave us a nice day."

"I've been praying for a good day. Not too hot. This feels perfect." He turned to the man who walked up beside him. "I want to introduce you to Miles. He's one of our neighbors, lives just a little bit outside of Raspberry Ridge on the northern side. His wife and my wife will be here shortly." Pastor Garnet paused, then said, "Actually they are pulling in now."

Pastor Garnet's eyes lit up as he looked toward his wife. He took a moment to watch as she drove and then said, "They're going to participate in the cooking class and make sure that we have plenty of water and anything else that we need. If I need someone to run to town for screws or anything else, she's going to do it for us."

"That's great. We have our own gofer."

"That's right. And she has Miles's wife with her. That's Norma Jean." He spoke as the lady stopped and got out of her car.

"Nice to meet you, Norma Jean." He'd already met Mertie, the pastor's wife, at church. She seemed like a nice lady and wholly suited to be a pastor's wife. She had the decorum but also seemed to have a sense of humor and a compassion for people, as well as an ability to roll with things. Like showing up for cooking class and a roofing session on Friday morning.

The ladies went on into the house, and he and the pastor and Miles stood and chatted for a bit about their plan of attack. Miles had done the most roofs, although the pastor had helped with some and Wesley had done some with his gramps back in the day. He hadn't put too many of the metal roofs on, because they weren't really a thing back when he was doing it.

As he thought, the roof went on quickly, with the ladies bringing out an occasional drink, and eventually delicious smells wafted out of the cottage as well.

"I think the cooking class is a success," Pastor Garnet said as they screwed on the last piece of metal.

They had a little bit of trim work to do, and the gutters needed to be attached, but the roof would not leak.

"As long as they get that out of the oven in time," Wesley said, knowing from experience that leaving something in too long totally negated any type of talent one might have when one was cooking.

"Speaking from experience, I presume," Miles said with a wink.

"I think you might have a little bit of that same experience," Wesley said, just judging from his expression.

"I cooked a few meals on my own, and I kept my daughter and myself from starving, but that's about all I can say about that."

"Inability to cook seems to be at epidemic levels here in Raspberry Ridge, and here at the Independent Bible Church, we are doing our best to fight that terrible, insidious encroachment upon our dietary sensitivities."

Pastor Garnet had used a fake radio voice starting out, but he kind of puttered out at the end, like he had run out of ideas. Which made it even funnier, and everyone was laughing as they climbed down from the roof.

"I really appreciate you guys giving me a hand with this."

"Not a problem. You just give me a call when the gutters come in, and I'll be out to give you a hand putting them up."

"I'll do that," he said, shaking Miles's hand, and then the pastor's as well, before they went to gather up a little bit of garbage that was lying around on the ground.

"Hey, guys, I was sent out here to see if you might be interested in stopping for lunch? I think it's gonna be pretty good. Grandma was teaching everyone to make her chicken divan, and I'm pretty sure it turned out really, really good." Birdie came out, an apron tied around her slender waist, a little flour on her nose.

"Does that take flour? Because I'm pretty sure I see something that resembles that substance on your face."

"I think you're trying to get me to tell you what we're having for dessert," she said, putting a hand on her hip and lifting a brow at him.

He liked her little sassy expression and the way she tossed her head.

"I might be."

"Smells like apple pie to me," Pastor Garnet said, walking by Wesley. "And if you're not going in, I can eat yours and mine too."

"Seems to me like the pastor is not used to physical labor and he worked himself up an appetite today," Wesley said, slapping Pastor Garnet on the back and exchanging a grin with Miles.

"I'm not allowing any defamation of the pastor in my house," Birdie said with a grin.

"See? She's gonna make you be nice there, Wesley. Now that I've done all the work for you."

"I did twice as much as you," Wesley said, following him into the kitchen and laughing when Birdie rolled her eyes.

"When are you boys ever going to grow up?"

"I'm mature," Miles said.

"He's just trying to get seconds on the apple pie," Wesley called over his shoulder.

Eleven

W esley had enjoyed himself, even though the work was hard and hot. Miles and Pastor Garnet were great guys to work with, and they had been joking around all day. That made the time go a lot faster, and it made the work a lot lighter.

Of course, his enjoyment of the day might have also had something to do with the fact that Birdie was inside. And he knew it.

She looked cool and fresh as she helped the other ladies finish setting the table. Gramps carried his masterpiece and set it down in the middle. Somehow, they'd made the table bigger, although Wesley had not figured out how. And then he realized that maybe they'd set a chair down on its side and thrown a tablecloth over top of it. And probably borrowed chairs from his house, because he thought the one looked familiar.

"Move out of the way, boys. This is the best chicken divan you've ever had."

"I sure hope you can replicate that, when you're back in your natural environment," Wesley muttered.

"Don't give me no lip, boy. This here's some good eatin'."

"We actually made two. I could see the worry in my husband's eyes as he looked around the table and then back at the dish." Mertie set the second pan on the table, right next to her husband.

"I believe I detect some favoritism here," Wesley said.

"Maybe you should become a man of the Word, and then the ladies will serve you like that," Pastor Garnet said with a smirk and then another sweet look at his wife who patted him on the shoulder.

They all settled around the table while the aroma of apple pie made Wesley's stomach growl. They must be in the oven. And he'd be willing to bet that there was gonna be ice cream to go along with it. Gram seemed to be able to align all those things perfectly. He wasn't quite sure how she did it.

"Knock knock?" a voice called from the door as they were all getting settled.

There was silence, and then Birdie jumped up from her chair where she was sitting across the table from Wesley.

"Becky! Perfect timing. We were about to begin. You were coming to eat, right?"

"I smelled the apple pie over my side of the hill, and I just followed my nose. I didn't realize it was going to be so crowded in here though."

"We always have room for one more. Come on in," Birdie said again, opening the door and waving Becky inside. While Birdie had been opening the door, her gram had jumped up and set another place on the table. They had used some kind of bench at the end, and her gram, who had been sitting on it, slid over to the side to make it a two-seater.

"You can sit right here. Plenty of room. The cooking class of the Independent Bible Church of Raspberry Ridge had their first lesson, and you can help us decide if I was successful in teaching these folks how to make chicken divan."

"I can do that, no problem. But it looks like there was some roofing going on as well."

"That was us. We just happened to schedule it for a day that the church was also having their cooking class," Pastor Garnet said seriously. "I always admire the Lord's good timing."

There were some murmurs and laughter around the table as Becky settled down and Birdie took her place across from Wesley again.

Pastor Garnet said grace, and they passed the food, with the conversation flowing, periodic laughter ringing out. Wesley had to admit that the food was delicious. Whether his gramps had actually made it or not, he wasn't convinced, because he'd never actually eaten anything that his gramps had made that was actually edible.

But he wanted to believe. Mostly because if the ladies ever went on a trip, he knew he wasn't going to starve.

"You know, Cassie Spokes, who is Doyle's housekeeper, has been thinking about starting a diner. I think you would be a good addition to that diner, Gram. You and she ought to get together."

"Oh, I don't know. I might be able to squeeze that into my schedule somehow. It sounds like fun. Maybe I will look her up. Does she go to church?"

"She's been there a couple of times, but she doesn't necessarily come on a regular basis. However, maybe we can change that as well as add a diner to the businesses in Raspberry Ridge."

"Becky is hoping to open a riding stable. Which would be another really great addition," Birdie said.

Wesley hadn't realized that, and he looked in surprise at the girl at the end of the table. She had been wearing boots with jeans and a regular T-shirt, with her hair in a ponytail. She looked young, but he figured she was probably mid-twenties.

"That's why I was here, actually. I told you I would let you know when I got my second saddle, and I have it if you're still interested in riding."

"I am."

"The best times to ride are dawn and dusk. Not only is it cooler for the horses, but you have a pretty sunrise and sunset to look at while you ride."

"Do you have enough horses? Because I wouldn't mind going?" Wesley couldn't believe that he had spoken up. And especially in front of all of the people. He hadn't exactly asked Birdie on a date, but he had shown some serious interest. He held his breath while she looked at him in surprise.

"I was under the impression that Becky was going to ride with me."

"The horses don't always like to go out by themselves. Sometimes you'll get a horse who doesn't mind, but the two I have now don't like to go out without the other one. It doesn't have to be me riding the other one. It could be the two of you going together."

"I need a crash course in riding, since it's been years since I sat on the back of a horse, and I don't remember much of anything else other than I'm supposed to stay there until it stops."

"That's right. Please stay seated until the rides come to a complete stop," Miles intoned like he was a teenager working at an amusement park ride.

"Sounds to me like you did that a time or two. Did you work at an amusement park as a kid?"

"I did. Not Disneyland though. Craig's Cruisers."

"Wow."

"Yeah. That's really all I got out of it though, the ability to tell people to stay still."

"That comes in handy when you're a parent, or so I understand," Pastor Garnet said.

"It might also come in handy if the pastor goes over time in church," Mertie said with a teasing smile at her husband.

"Now that I know that there is someone in the congregation who can do that, I don't have to make sure I let everyone out on time." He paused and then looked around the table with narrowed eyes. "On time is one o'clock, right?"

Laughter rang around the table as the buzzer for the oven went off.

"Oh! That's for me," Gramps exclaimed and then hopped up from his seat.

"Don't forget to use oven mitts," Norma Jean said softly as Gramps opened the oven without picking anything up with which to take his pies out.

"Thanks. I made that mistake once. I shouldn't be making it a second time."

There were some glances exchanged around the table, and a couple of the ladies had smirks on their faces, but nobody said anything else. Until finally, Gram said, "What happens in Raspberry Ridge Independent Bible Church's culinary class stays in Raspberry Ridge Independent Bible Church's culinary class."

Everyone laughed, although Wesley was going to have to get the real story out of Gramps when they got home. Had he burned his fingers?

Regardless, the air smelled glorious, and Wesley rethought his decision to get a second helping, when it might mean that he would only get one piece of pie before he couldn't eat anything more.

Mertie had gotten up to get the ice cream out of the freezer, and Birdie had stood and started taking away the plates of the people who were finished eating the chicken.

"Eyes bigger than your stomach?" she said as she walked by him, leaving his plate.

"No. Buyer's remorse, I think, since something better came along after I got this."

"We made one for you to take home, so no worries."

"You are a good neighbor. The best," Wesley said as she gave him another smile before walking away.

He had enjoyed the day, even though the work had been hard, because the company had been good.

He ended up leaving with Gramps shortly after everyone had eaten pie, without talking to Birdie again. He wasn't sure whether they were still going to meet along the beach, but he hoped so.

Twelve

"I almost texted and asked if you were coming, and then I saw you walking out, and it was perfect timing because I had just picked up my notebook."

That was how Birdie greeted him as they stepped out on the beach together, each of them going down the steps in front of their house and walking toward each other. They had a tendency to meet in the middle and then go down and sit on dry sand, as close to the water as they could get without getting wet.

It wasn't like the ocean where the tide was shifting all day long. Although there was a slight tide, it wasn't extremely noticeable. Which made it nice. A person didn't have to constantly be moving their beach chair. Except neither one of them brought chairs; they'd both been sitting on the sand.

"Thank you so much for the delicious food and the pie you sent home with us. Everything was so good," Wesley said, putting a hand on his stomach. "I almost took a nap instead of coming out here today, but it was the idea of the good company I would be missing that got me out the door."

"You are welcome to go back and take a nap if you want to. No one says that we have to write every single day. And I know for me, the things I have to do are coming along quite nicely."

"Me too." And it's true, they were. He was definitely ahead.

She knew he was writing an autobiography, but he still wasn't sure what she was writing.

They had an unspoken rule between them that neither one of them asked about the other, but he'd been thinking about it a little bit.

"So I feel like I have a little bit of an affinity with you because both of us are hiding something. Can I say that?"

She pursed her lips together and narrowed her eyes, looking at the lake and seeming to ponder this question. He thought she was just goofing, but he wasn't sure. She hadn't broached the subject at all, and neither had he. More out of respect for her than because he still wanted to keep his identity a secret from her. He was pretty sure that she would keep it for him. That he didn't have to worry about her spilling it without his permission.

"You can say that. As long as you don't ask me what I'm hiding."

"How do you know I haven't figured it out?"

"I think there will be signs if you do," she said thoughtfully but with a little smile on her face, so he knew she wasn't being totally serious.

"That big, huh?"

"No. Not necessarily. I think I'll just know."

"Have you figured me out?"

"Maybe," she said, but he thought she really hadn't. She had said she had no idea who he was, and she hadn't put a lot of effort in figuring it out. "Is it terrible that I really don't want to know? I mean, I am curious, but," she put her hand out fast when he started to open his mouth, "I really don't want to know. I just like not knowing. Is that terrible?"

"No. I think it will probably change things if the truth comes out. And the more people who know, the more likely it is that someone who isn't supposed to know will find out, and then everything will go downhill from there."

"I agree. Although, tomorrow is the day that we're supposed to watch the twins. Are you ready?"

"I thought we were watching six kids?" he said, knowing that he really had no clue what he signed up for.

"Yeah, I guess it's the twins that have me concerned though. They're not that old, and I think it would take a lot of attention."

"Will Vera be helping us?"

"I think since there's two of us, she and Dominic are going to do some maintenance work on the healing garden. It's kind of like a date for them."

"Wow. So we're trusted to have the children alone without their parents?"

"I believe so. I think they thought we would actually show up. I do think there are people who sign up for it and then don't show."

"That's too bad."

They didn't say anything for a bit, just looking at the water and enjoying the nice day, when he said, "This is the best week of writing I've had. I just wanted to thank you again for pushing me into it."

"I pushed you into it?" she asked.

He was pretty sure she knew he was teasing. "You know what I mean. I was trying to be a little bit serious. I do appreciate you."

"I appreciate you, too. Although, I think it's going to be a couple of days until we have another day to write."

"Maybe we should take the weekends off. Give us a break from being creative."

"You're not going to have a break from me. Because we're doing the kids together tomorrow, but you have a break from writing."

"I don't need a break from you. You've been growing on me."

"I see. I think it's the apple pie that's been growing on you, and that's my gram."

"Hmm. She's modest. I like it." They chuckled together. She wiggled her bare toes into the sand, and he did, too, loving the way it felt as it ran through his toes, the soft warmth, the day with no pressure. Even the idea of watching six kids tomorrow wasn't terrible. Because Birdie would be there too. And one thing he figured out with Birdie, he would have a good time with her.

And that made him look forward to it.

"So what do you know about Becky?" Wesley asked after a few minutes of silence where he looked down at his laptop.

"I just saw her at church, went over, and chatted with her. She said she was trying to start a riding stable, and I felt a little bit bad for her, so I asked if I could be her first customer. Well, I also love horses but haven't had much opportunity to ride."

"All right. So I know you're not a famous American jockey."

"You're right. I'm not." She looked down. "I think I weigh about one hundred pounds too much."

"I don't think we should talk about your weight. That makes me nervous." Wesley gave a fake shiver which made her laugh.

"So I guess we have that tomorrow too. I kind of forgot about it. I'm looking forward to it, but I'm a little nervous."

"Nervous?"

"I'm afraid I might fall off."

"I think if you just hold onto that little thing that sticks up on the saddle, you really can't go wrong."

"Maybe we could just lead the horses for a walk on the beach; we could just all four take a walk together."

"You can lead your horse if you want to, but I'm lazy."

She laughed. "I'm thinking that's not true. You guys did a great job on the roof. I can't say whether or not it leaks, since we haven't had any rain, but it looks nice."

"Think there's some rain in the forecast for Sunday, so maybe we'll get it tested out then."

After a little bit of talking with Birdie before they started writing, it seemed like his words just flowed. He had the best writing day he had all week, finishing an entire chapter.

"Thanks for meeting me. I probably should scoot. Gram's going to be home soon from the nursing home and ready to start supper."

"I think I'll work another week, and then...would you be willing to read what I've written?" he asked, knowing his words were unsure. He'd been sitting there thinking about asking her for a while.

"I can. Are you sure?"

He nodded. "I trust you. I know that you know how it is to not want your name out there, and so I know that you're not going to rat me out, if you figure it out. But since I'm writing the book in first person, you might not."

"All right. So we have one more week of anonymity, and then I might know who you are."

"And I might figure you out as well."

That's kind of how they always left it. Just them teasing each other that they were going to figure out who the other one was, but he didn't really think they would. Maybe when she read what he had written for his autobiography she'd figure it out.

They got up and walked together for a little bit before they needed to separate and go to their separate steps.

"Tomorrow morning at nine?" he said as they stopped and looked at each other.

"Tomorrow morning at nine," she repeated.

He was most definitely looking forward to it.

Thirteen

"So have you ever done anything with children before?" Wesley asked as they pulled out from the cottage and motored slowly down the sandy road toward the main street. It would only be about a five-minute drive, if that, until they made it to Vera and Dominic's house.

"Not really," Birdie said, her fingers twisting in her lap. "You?" She looked over at him, and he couldn't misread the hope in her eyes.

"Zilch. I didn't even have siblings."

"That's great. So, you've never changed a diaper?" she asked, and he thought she was probably trying to sound cheerful.

"I have not. Hopefully that doesn't change today."

"Well, it's going to change for one of us, I'm pretty sure."

"You've never changed a diaper either?"

She shook her head.

"What famous person has never changed a diaper," he said, teasing, scratching his chin as though he were trying to figure it out.

He felt the several days' worth of beard on his face and thought that he probably ought to shave, although that was part of his disguise. One of his biggest sponsors was a razor company, and he appeared in a lot of commercials. The scruff on his cheeks would hopefully be helpful in keeping him incognito.

"I think it would have been a bigger hint if I had changed a diaper. There are fewer famous people to choose from that way."

He laughed, agreeing with her assessment. "Well, it's only for two hours."

"Yes. That's what I heard too. Apparently Vera hasn't been out since her C-section."

"I've heard those take a long time to recover from, not that I know. Or will ever find out," he said, wanting to put a hand on his stomach in sympathetic pain.

"That's what I've heard too." She couldn't believe that Dominic and Vera were going to entrust their six children to them. Her grandma must have been a pretty smooth talker in order to have that happen. Regardless, her nerves were pinging as they pulled into the Millers' house.

"I'm not sure I'm ready for this," Wesley said, echoing her exact thoughts as they stopped on the drive and he kept his hands on the wheel.

"There's still time to turn around and leave," she said, scrunching up her face and thinking that if he was going to agree with her, she would have a hard time getting out of the car anyway.

"There is." He nodded, looking straight ahead at the garage door that was down. "Can we live with ourselves if we do that?"

"I think I can," she said. "I think that would be easier than changing a diaper, anyway."

"I'm not going to disagree with you." He tapped the steering wheel. "Are we going to do the hard thing or the easy thing? We could make this a skip day, go to the beach, and hang out."

"Or we can go in and do our best to wrangle six children, including two newborns, when neither one of us have any experience with children and don't even know how to change diapers."

"That makes the skip day look really, really nice."

"It does, doesn't it?" They sat there for about three seconds, and then, almost as though their brains were working in tandem, they reached for their door latches and yanked them so close together that it was just one sound.

They looked across the seats at each other and grinned.

"We can do this."

"Or we'll die trying," she said with a dramatic flair.

They walked up to the door and knocked.

As though he was waiting for them on the other side, Dominic opened it almost immediately.

"We were afraid you're going to chicken out. It took you a little bit longer than strictly necessary to get out of the car."

"Do people do that?"

"Yesterday's person did," Vera said, smiling as she came walking toward them. "And they weren't even going to be watching the twins, just the four older kids."

Behind both of them, kids zoomed around, flying one way and then the other, and Wesley didn't even try to keep track of them. He was going to be hard put to just keep the kids alive, let alone learn their names.

"I have a paper on the counter with our phone numbers on it. We're only going to be down at the healing garden, and I'm just going to be watching my husband do a few little maintenance things."

"And we will be back in two hours, no more," Dominic added, putting a hand on his wife's shoulder and saying his words firmly, as though wanting to reassure them that they were not going to be stuck with their children forever.

It wasn't a huge amount of reassurance for Birdie, but she glanced at Wesley and returned his tremulous smile.

"Everyone should be fine. The twins have just been fed. They're down for a nap right now and in their dual pack and play, right here with the rest of the kids. So you don't have to try to keep track of them in some room somewhere," Vera said, leading them over to where the twins slept in a side-by-side bassinet type thing.

"If they do wake up, I have instructions for formula and the diapers are right there," she pointed to the diapers, "and if you have any questions, you can call us. Honestly, at this point, we'll be happy if we can just have five minutes outside of the house."

"Together. Five minutes together," Dominic added.

"As for the other kids, don't worry about them. They can do whatever they want to except watch TV. They can play, inside or outside, we let them run in the house, we originally started with the rule that you couldn't, and we decided that we didn't want to go insane, so we quit telling everyone to stop running after having them for about an hour and a half."

"Yeah, that's about right," Dominic said, looking at his wife and nodding.

"I'm not sure if it kept us actually sane, but it was a nice idea."

"Yeah. I have noticed you're a little on the crazy side."

"You mean you didn't notice that when I said yes when you asked me to marry you?"

"Oh, that's right. I was looking for someone like you."

They grinned at each other, and then Vera looked back at them. "I'm sorry. He's sidetracking me. Do you have any questions?"

"So, we don't have to feed them, don't have to change them, all we have to do is keep them from killing each other for two hours?"

"Yeah. That's pretty much the baseline," Dominic said. "That's my life in a nutshell right now. Survive, without killing the children."

Dominic and Vera looked at each other, nodded and shrugged, and then glanced back at them, to see whether or not they thought of any questions.

Birdie was quiet, she looked a little shell-shocked, as her eyes got caught on a little girl who ran through the house with white leotards on. Wesley looked again. Scratch that. She had no leotards on.

Possibly his expression was a mirror of Birdie's.

"Oh. We also try to keep the house from catching on fire," Dominic said, and then they disappeared out the door.

"Well, if I'd known that to begin with, it would have changed everything," Wesley said as he stared at the closed door, feeling a little bit like it was a prison cell that had just closed in front of him.

"Same. Wow. Keep them alive and keep the house from burning down. I don't know how they expect two humans to accomplish such lofty heights." Her eyes narrowed, and she leaned toward him, lowering her voice. "The one girl is naked."

"Was that a girl?" he said.

"Didn't you have biology in school?" she asked.

He snorted. "I think I was in the gym."

She laughed out loud at that, and he almost thought she was going to touch his bicep, but she didn't. "I like it."

Somehow her words made a soft thrill expand in his chest, more than the syrupy compliments that he got from numerous girls about everything from his play on the ice to his biceps to his white teeth.

"So do you think we ought to go in and interrupt their play and try to learn their names and introduce ourselves and all that?" Birdie asked as her eyes scanned over the room again where a truck rumbled past, followed by a boy running, and then a ball zoomed through.

"I think that's going to be the straw that breaks the camel's back. If we want to get through this without anyone dying, and the house not going up in flames, I think we need to focus. Zero in on what's really important."

"Gotcha. So we just stand here. We're referees."

"As long as you're fair," he said automatically.

She jerked her head over at him, and he pressed his lips closed, gave her a tight-lipped smile, and looked back at the kids.

"So, what's going to make us call the parents?" she asked.

"If either one of those things over there make a sound," he nodded at the sleeping babies, "I'm dialing their number immediately. Both at the same time if necessary."

"Agreed."

"Anything else?"

"Any kind of explosion."

"Right. Explosions definitely require a call to the parents. What about you?" he asked.

"I would feel better if the girl put her clothes on, but...that's probably not parent worthy since she had them off before they left."

"I'm not sure they saw that. I think they were just afraid that you and I were going to chicken out, and they were more concerned about getting out the door before we did. After all, if they're out first, we can't leave until they come back."

"Good point."

"Blood. Any blood, definitely a call to the parents."

"Right. One of us will call the parents, one of us will call 911."

"Good thinking. I feel like we have a plan now."

They turned and watched the children. It felt like complete chaos, but after a while, he thought he had figured out that there were two boys and two girls.

It took about five minutes, but on one trip through, one girl zoomed around them, her long skirt flowing from her waist, and she was wearing what looked like another skirt on her head, maybe to imitate hair, but Wesley wasn't entirely sure. Perhaps she thought she was some kind of forested creature. Regardless, she didn't stop moving, but she looked them both in the eye and said, "I'm Emma." Then she zoomed away.

"All right. That's easy. Emma has clothes on," Birdie murmured, mostly to herself.

"As long as she doesn't take them off, I think we're good."

"She seemed like maybe she had put on what her sister had taken off, although I'm not sure about that."

He hadn't considered that. That her hairpiece might have come from her sister's bottom.

"I have to pee," the smallest child said as he ran up to them, holding himself.

They looked at each other. His panic was probably mirrored on Birdie's face.

"I think this is yours," he said, hoping that she was not going to argue.

"It's your gender. I think you need to take care of it."

She had him there. Actually, he could argue, but what if the little girl came up and needed to go to the bathroom? Would that be his turn? No, definitely it was better to deal with the little boy—

"Too late." The little boy shrugged his shoulders and went running off.

"It's still yours," Birdie said.

"I had no idea that you were so devoid of any type of compassion or consideration for your fellow man."

"I think my compassion will come back after you have those pants changed."

"Me?"

"He puts them on the same way you do, one leg at a time."

"I wouldn't be so sure about that. He looks like the type of kid that probably jumps into his jeans in the morning."

But as he watched the little kid run around, there was definitely a wet spot in the front and going down the inside of both legs.

Birdie did not look like she was going to be the slightest bit of help, and he couldn't blame her. He actually wasn't sure which would be harder, watching the other five children while he took the one kid out of commission and changed his pants, or changing the pants on the one.

"First things first. I need to catch him."

"I would hold him at arm's length if I were you. At least until you get the wet stuff off."

"Thanks for the advice there, partner."

"Not a problem, Jack."

He wasn't sure where that came from, but the way she said it made him laugh.

"The next catastrophe is yours, Jill."

She grinned at his retort and seemed to accept the nickname that he christened her with without comment.

It seemed kind of apt, since they were trying to keep their identities a secret, that they would have cutesy names.

He was able to swoop in and grab the little guy with the wet pants, but his next problem was how to get him somewhere to get them changed. And where to go?

"We're gonna change your pants, kiddo," he said.

"No!" the boy yelled and then started squirming in his arms.

That was unexpected. He expected the kids to peacefully comply, not stage an insurrection immediately.

Right. Plan B.

"Emma," he called.

The little girl with the skirt on her bottom and another skirt on her head came running out of what he assumed must be the playroom.

"What?" she asked as she did a lap around him, both of her skirts flying in the breeze.

"Where are the clothes for this one?" he asked, nodding to the squirming child who was doing his best to pull a Houdini in his arms.

"Follow me!" she said as she did a second lap around him and then cut off, kind of like a car at a roundabout, down a hallway.

"Could you go slower?" he asked, trying to hold the little boy at arm's length and still keep up to Emma.

"I'm fast!" Emma said, running back down the hall, doing a lap around him, and then swinging back like a boomerang and disappearing to the left at the end of the hall.

He heard thundering beside his ear and realized that she had taken the stairs. That made sense. The bedrooms were probably upstairs.

"If you would stop squirming, this would be a lot easier."

"No! No! No!"

It was kind of like having a political discussion with someone who had no facts to back up their opinion. Wesley laughed at the very apt description as he made the turn and started up the stairs, careful not to allow the child's feet to drag but also very careful not to let any wet part touch any part of his body. He had not volunteered for this, but he would gamely do his best, except...he drew the line at bodily fluids. Particularly the bodily fluids that came out the bottom end.

Except, he didn't exactly want to get puked on either, so bodily fluids, big red line in the sand.

esley had made it to the top of the steps when some kind of crash echoed from below. He stopped, listening, and two seconds later, a scream and then loud crying broke out.

"Jill?" he called down the stairs.

"I'm on it, Jack." Her voice came up the stairs, calm, a bit humorous over using their new nicknames, but also with a slight edge, not panic, but perhaps concentration.

"Roger that, Jill."

It was a little bit juvenile, but he was still getting a kick out of it, and he needed to do something to stay sane. He could understand now why Dominic and Vera had practically run out the door.

He wasn't sure he was going to stick around and talk when they came back. And he sure hoped that Birdie hopped quickly in the car beside him, because he wasn't quite sure how long he was going to be waiting in the driveway for her to get in.

Maybe he should warn her.

"These are his," Emma said as she flew by him, throwing pants in his face and thundering back down the stairs, her skirts flying.

"I need underwear!"

No reply, but soon she was thundering back up the stairs and running back into one of the rooms.

It wasn't long after that that the underwear came flying at his head the same way the pants had.

"Thanks," he said, wondering where in the world Dominic had gotten his children.

He knew that they were adopted, and he admired Vera and Dominic for their...bravery. Yes. That was the right word. Bravery. Probably they hadn't met the children before they adopted them.

Yeah. That explained a lot.

That was the story that he was going to stick with, because he couldn't imagine someone being so...crazy that they would meet these kids and decide to adopt them anyway.

But he thought about kids growing up without a mom or dad, being shuffled from house to house, and maybe not even staying with their siblings, how scary and hard that would be. He thought about the commitment of taking a child into a person's home and saying that you would be their parent for the rest of their life.

And then doing that four times over. And then, having twins on top of everything else.

Wow. He could hardly believe that Vera and Dominic had willingly sacrificed so much of their lives for these kids.

He wondered if they'd ever appreciate it. He certainly didn't expect them to appreciate it now, not their age, but... Someday maybe?

He hoped so. They definitely had his respect.

It was a bit of a wrestling match to get the wet pants off and the dry pants on. He recalled his high school wrestling matches and recalled again why he had chosen hockey as his game, just hit something, there was no trying to roll it around and finesse it into little holes.

Of course, that wasn't exactly a description of wrestling either, but it aptly described what he was trying to do with the kid and his pants.

He had the underwear on, when he realized it was on backward, and he honestly wondered if Vera and Dominic would notice. Guessing that they wouldn't, he decided to leave it like that. And struggled to get the pants over top of them.

Remembering that there had been a crash downstairs, he pinned down the flailing arms with one arm and grabbed the flailing legs with the other arm and took the struggling kid downstairs.

"There you go," he said at the bottom of the stairs, setting his charge free. The kid didn't waste any time in running away from him, although he did stop about four good strides away and turned around and yelled, "Don't you ever do that again!"

"Tell me a little sooner before you have to go to the bathroom next time," he called to the retreating back.

It was these children who were running around church, and he realized now what a small miracle it had been for Vera and Dominic to actually get them to all sit in the pew together and behave themselves.

He felt like he just survived a war, and he still had...he checked his phone...one hour and forty-seven minutes left.

That was if Vera and Dominic came back on time, which after being here for thirteen minutes, Wesley highly doubted.

As he walked into the living room, he realized what the crash had been.

The large flat-screen TV lay precariously propped against the wall, while the stand that it'd been on looked like someone had started to make tinder wood out of it.

Birdie glanced up from where she was tentatively trying to put it back together. "No fires, Jack."

He snorted. "Wow. And I thought they were joking."

He wondered if the TV had survived the crash, but there was no point in trying to figure it out until they got the stand put back up. Why didn't they have their TV hung on the wall like normal people?

Hopefully because they never watched it.

"One hour and forty-six minutes left, Jill. But who's counting, right?"

"Kids or stand, Jack. Your choice."

"Stand." He didn't need to think about that one.

"I'm not sure whether to thank you or be mad at you," she said as she sighed, looking at the stand, which seemed like an impossible task to try to put back together.

"If you would have taken Wet Pants, this wouldn't have happened," he said, loading his tone with lots of snark.

It made her laugh, as he thought it would.

So, this was not going to be an easy thing, but he was pretty sure it was going to be a fun thing. As whatever he seemed to do with Birdie was. Their banter felt easy, and no matter how dorky he was, she didn't roll her eyes and act like he was a loser.

They exchanged a look as she pushed herself off the ground, and he surveyed the broken stand.

He didn't think that Vera and Dominic would be the slightest bit surprised or upset about either that or the TV set.

"If I had some tools, I think I could get it put back together fairly decently, but I'll do my best."

"All right, then I'll go back to making sure the children don't kill themselves or set the house on fire."

He was pretty sure that Vera and Dominic were probably trying to train their children, but with the fact that Vera had been pregnant with twins not long after they had adopted the kids, it probably made it very difficult. He was no expert on pregnancy, but he was guessing that Vera had a lot more on her hands than what she had been expecting when they had adopted the children.

Regardless, it was best to patch the stand back together, and then, rather than setting the TV back on top of it, he set it in the corner, with the flat screen toward the wall.

Hopefully out of the way where the children wouldn't knock it down.

By the time Vera and Dominic had come back, he was ready to lie down and sleep for the rest of the day.

Thankfully, the twins had not woken up, and Vera and Dominic did not seem the slightest bit surprised or upset about the TV stand, the wet pants, or even the possibility of their TV being broken.

"We never use it anyway," Dominic said as he shrugged a shoulder. "As long as the kids weren't hurt."

"No. They're fast, and they got out from underneath it before it fell."

"I should put it on the wall anyway," Dominic said, giving Vera a look, which she returned.

"Or we could give it away. We never watch it anyway."

They turned back to Wesley and Birdie. "I know they're a handful. I really appreciate you coming. I...understand if you don't volunteer to come back."

"I think we'll be back. We had a good time, didn't we, Jack?"

Wesley decided that he was not as good a liar as what she was. "If you say so, Jill."

"Oh, stop," she said, grinning and rolling her eyes as he opened the door and she threw up a hand to wave goodbye.

They walked out into the bright sunshine, and he couldn't help but feel like he had been released from prison, except, as he opened the car door, he realized that maybe he would miss prison after all.

Or maybe prison wasn't so bad when you had the right cellmate.

They got in and sat down in the car, both of them just sitting there, exhausted.

"We survived," he said in a monotone.

"No one died," she said in the exact same tone.

"The house didn't burn down."

"Success, Jack," she said, lifting up her hand and holding her fist over the console.

He grinned, bumping her fist and starting the car. "What time are we supposed to be at the stable for horseback riding?"

"I think seven or so. She said a two-hour ride should let us see the sunset."

"I'm gonna sleep until then."

"I hope I can. I'm not sure what Gram has planned for today, but I know she's doing something."

"I guess if I see you with your blanket out on the beach, I'll know she's got some kind of meeting going on in your house."

"Yeah. Don't disturb," she said, laughing.

"After the last two hours, I can guarantee you that I will leave you alone."

He had to be honest though; he couldn't leave her thinking that it had been terrible.

"Were you serious about saying that it wasn't that bad?" he said as he pulled off the main road in Raspberry Ridge and onto the sandy road that took them to the cottages.

"Mostly because of you. It seems like whatever we do together, I have a good time. I had to admit, after the TV crash I wasn't so sure I was going to make it the two hours, but you done good, Jack."

"That's funny, because as we were walking out the door, I felt like I'd been released from prison, only I knew I was going to miss it because I had such a great cellmate."

"Are you talking about me? Or the kid with the wet pants?"

"I think he didn't like me, did he?"

"He was pretty violent toward you, but he did seem to have an affinity for you as well."

"I think he could grow on me."

"That's why I said what I did. It wasn't as bad as what I thought it was going to be, and... If I have a year to think about it, I might even go back." She sounded surprised.

"Think it will take me about five years, but same."

As he pulled into her cottage, he said, "Looks like you got the place to yourself."

The Ferrari was gone, and she nodded. "I better slip my nap in while I can."

"I might eat before I get mine. That chicken divan was really good, and I think there might be a piece of apple pie left if Gramps didn't eat it in the last two hours."

"Let me know if he did. I think there's some left over at my house too."

"I knew there was a reason I kept you around," he joked.

"I know. My gram. She's my male magnet."

With that, she got out of the car, and he was still laughing as he drove to his cottage.

Are we riding together?

Birdie sent a text to Wesley, since she hadn't had the foresight to talk about it before she got out of the car earlier. She was just happy to have survived the children and was really looking forward to a rest. She had no idea how Vera and Dominic did that day in and day out, and the twins were just babies. They had years more work ahead of them. The idea made her want to crawl into a hole.

But she also admired the fact that Vera and Dominic had obviously given up what could have been a life of ease and luxury to take four children and try to give them a good stable homelife. They'd obviously been undisciplined wherever they had grown up originally and possibly even encouraged to run wild. Vera and Dominic certainly had their hands full trying to turn them into productive citizens, and again she had to hand it to them for choosing the difficult path when they could have enjoyed a life of ease and luxury.

Was that what she was doing? Enjoying her life of ease and luxury?

The thought wasn't a good one, as she considered what she had done with her life. Of course she had donated more money each year than most people saw in a lifetime to various charities, but... What kind of manpower had she put in?

When had she ever lifted a finger to try to make the world a better place by her own sweat, blood, and tears?

There were so many children in the foster system who could use good parents who cared about them, and yet she had never even considered looking at children who needed to be adopted.

She felt guilty about it and knew it was something that she was going to want to think about and possibly change in her own life. *But not today*, she thought as her phone buzzed with a text and she looked at it on the sink where it was sitting as she fixed her hair from her nap.

We can. I'll pick you up?

Sure. Five minutes?

Whenever you want. I'm sitting outside the cottage.

She hated to keep people waiting, so she threw the comb down, figuring it didn't matter at all what her hair looked like, because they were just horseback riding. It was going to get messed up anyway because there was always a lake breeze.

"He's outside waiting," her gram said.

"I know. He just texted me."

"If he were a gentleman, he'd come in. You don't expect your date to run out of the house and get in your car."

"I—"

"I'm here," Wesley said as she started to respond to her grandma. He gave a perfunctory knock on the door as he pushed it open.

"We're not going on a date, Gram. He doesn't have to come in and get me or meet my parents, or anything like that." Goodness, she was so far beyond that it wasn't even funny.

Gram ignored her. "That's a good boy. I was hoping I would see you. Just for that, I ought to send over another apple pie. You be sure to stop in here when you're bringing her back."

"It's going to be after dark, ma'am. But I'll definitely stop in. I'll do a lot for apple pie."

"I'm glad you enjoyed it," she said with a smile.

Birdie wasn't sure whether Wesley had told her he enjoyed it or Gramps had mentioned it. She seemed to be spending a lot of time with Gramps, who had been doing all of her running around with her.

If Gramps wasn't careful, Gram would have him signed up for all the things she was. Somebody should warn him.

"Text me if you need me, Gram," she said as she grabbed her sneakers and hurried out the door, figuring she could stick them on in the car.

"I can wait for you to put your shoes on. I didn't mean to rush you. Maybe I was hoping to get a slice of pie while I was waiting."

She almost screeched to a stop as she hit the bottom step. And turned slowly. "Really? I didn't even think about that. I just thought I didn't want to hold you up. I hate it when I'm supposed to be somewhere, and I have to sit around and wait on people."

He lifted a shoulder, casual and relaxed. "It depends on where you're waiting. In a hospital waiting room, yeah. In somebody's kitchen who happens to be one of the best apple pie makers in the entire world? It's not so hard."

"I like you made that distinction. I'll have to remember that. When you show up early when we're doing something together, it's not because you want to spend extra time with me. It's because you want to eat my gram's pie."

"I thought we agreed earlier that your gram was the male magnet."

"I guess we did," she said, sighing like it had been a trial.

"Here. The least I can do is open your door, since you're carrying your shoes."

"Why thank you, Jack," she said, tempted to salute before she got in, but she just smirked at him instead.

They'd spent enough time together that she felt completely at home with him and was actually looking forward to going on the horse ride, even though she was worried that she might fall off.

She was working on getting her shoes on when he got in.

"Are you still nervous?" he asked as he started the car and backed out.

"Mostly about falling off and getting hurt. You know, the older I get, the more concerned I get about that. When I was a kid, it didn't even occur to me that I should be worried about it."

"It's funny the things we don't think about when we're kids. I was reminded of pretty much every single thing today while we were watching those four...children."

He said the word "children" delicately, almost as though he felt like the word didn't apply. She knew he was just kidding, and she laughed.

"Honestly, what Vera and Dominic are doing is inspiring. Difficult, hard, and I'm not sure I would ever want to do it, but very inspiring. Those kids needed a home. You can just look at them and see how badly they do. And they weren't easy kids to take."

"And there are four of them!"

"Exactly. It wasn't like they were adopting two, which would be reasonable. But four?"

"And then they have twins on top of it!" she said as she lifted her other foot up to put the second shoe on.

"I definitely think they needed the help."

"Yeah. It actually made me feel really good to do it, even though it was...interesting, at the time."

She noticed at that point that he was wearing boots, and she looked at the tennis shoes she just put on.

"I don't own boots." She grimaced and looked over at him. "You think that's going to be a problem?"

"Yeah. Thou shall not ride horses unless thou ownest cowboy boots," he said.

"Oh my goodness. You're such a cracker head," she said, rolling her eyes. And then she narrowed them and looked over at him. "You *can* ride horses without boots on, right?"

"I'm sure people probably have ridden them barefoot. Although, I think it will hurt if you get your foot stepped on."

"True. So, I'm good? She's not going to turn me away?"

"I highly doubt it. Not her first customer."

"True. I would have quite the distinction." And then she gasped.

"What?" he asked, looking around, trying to figure out the source of her distress.

"What if she wants to take pictures? What if she wants to use us as an advertisement? Oh my goodness. I never even thought about that!" She felt like getting out of the car right there. How was she going to tell Becky that she couldn't do that?

"Becky hasn't said anything about that, has she?"

"No, but it's just common sense. You want to take pictures of happy people at your business so that it makes other people look at them and think 'Oh, I'll be happy like those happy people if I go to that business.'"

"You *are* a marketing exec. I thought you were." He nodded his head. "What famous marketing execs do I know?"

"Exactly zero," she said. "Because they're boring."

"Ouch. Somebody has a problem with marketing execs."

"No. I was just kidding, mostly. But I'm not a marketing exec, so you can stop thinking about it."

"Well, you're writing all those little jingles in your book, so if they're not marketing material—"

"Stop thinking about that." She heard the warning in her tone, but it was laced with humor, so she thought she was okay.

"All right. You're off the hook for today. But tomorrow, I'm going to start thinking about it again. Because you won't be sitting beside me telling me to stop. If you sit beside me in church, I might put it off for yet another day."

"Was that your backhanded way of asking me to sit beside you in church? Because if it was, your technique could use a little bit of improvement."

"So that's a no?" He grinned. "That's good, because I was hoping I could figure out—"

"That wasn't a no. I was just critiquing you and finding you lacking."

"Ouch."

"That's okay. You can keep practicing on me. I'll be sure to tell you my honest opinion."

"Don't hold back," he said, giving her an exaggerated cautious glance.

He put his turn signal on to turn down the lane to the farm that Becky was renting.

"I really would like to see Becky succeed, but I'm afraid she's just not going to have the customers that she's hoping she's going to back here."

"I'm not disagreeing with you. This is a hard place to try to get a business started."

They didn't say anything more as they drove slowly down the bumpy dirt road, until the dilapidated house and then the even more dilapidated barn came into view.

Two horses were saddled and tied to the hitching post in front of the barn.

"Wow. Do you think those are our horses?" Birdie breathed as they came to a stop at what they thought constituted the parking area in front of the barn.

"That's a gorgeous tail. It's dragging on the ground!"

"And the mane. Look how long it is." The horse turned so that it was a little bit diagonal toward them, and the wind lifted the ends of the mane which hung almost down to its knees.

"I've never seen a horse with a mane that long!"

"And that color. It looks like a steel gray. Such an odd color for a horse, but gorgeous."

They sat looking for a moment until Becky appeared in the barn and they realized that they needed to get out and stop staring.

"Remain seated until the ride stops," Wesley said as he yanked his door open, looking over at her with his eyebrows lifted like he was giving her last-minute instructions.

"Don't fall off," she said, keeping her instructions short and simple.

"That's my goal."

"Mine too."

They got out and walked over to Becky, who stood beside the horses.

"I didn't think you guys would mind if I saddled them up for you."

"I appreciate it. Looks like you've groomed them as well," Birdie said, running an eye over the second horse which was just as gorgeous as the first.

"What color is that? Some kind of gray?"

"It's called blue roan. It's actually a base coat of black, with enough white hairs to make the coat appear blue."

"Neat," Wesley said, nodding his head and running his eyes over the horses.

"They're so pretty. Picture-perfect."

"Speaking of pictures—"

"Actually," Wesley interrupted her. "We were hoping that we could ask you to not take pictures. Or if you're going to take pictures, to...not include our faces."

"Sure," Becky said, looking a little puzzled but seeming to shrug it off. "So it's okay if I take pictures? If I get your faces in them, I'll either blur them out or not use those pictures. Will that be okay?"

"That's fine with me," Birdie said, thinking that no one was going to recognize the shape of her body, which looked like every other woman out there. Thankfully she didn't have any distinctive tattoos. And she hadn't worn any kind of jewelry that might be recognizable either. Plus, she was wearing the old jeans and shirts that she bought at the secondhand store, so there was nothing she wore that anyone would recognize.

Wesley seemed to be the same, because he nodded. "That's a deal."

"All right." Becky said. "I won't post anything without you guys' approval."

That was fair, and Birdie hoped that eventually she would be able to post whatever she wanted to. Perhaps their names would bring people to her stable and cause it to be a success.

Birdie didn't want to be arrogant, but she was a pretty big deal. She was guessing that Wesley was too, whatever sphere he hailed from.

"All right, I have some forms I need you guys to sign," Becky said, walking back into the barn and motioning for Wesley and Birdie to follow her.

"I got cash out, because I assumed you probably didn't take cards," Wesley said as they walked into the barn.

Birdie was happy that he had thought about that and taken care of it, because she hadn't given it a thought. She almost told him, but Becky was talking about what the form said and then how much they would owe, and all Birdie did was sign on the dotted line, knowing that she was basically saying that if she got hurt, she wouldn't hold Becky liable. She didn't need to put a signature on a piece of paper to know that.

It was her choice to ride the horses.

Then, for the next ten minutes or so, Becky talked about how to mount and dismount, which side to use, and how to hold the reins.

"Both of these are mares that were supposed to be used for breeding, but they didn't work out for some reason. Either they couldn't be bred, or they couldn't carry a pregnancy full term."

"That's sad. They're so beautiful," Birdie murmured.

"Sad for them, but good for me. People enjoy riding pretty horses."

"I sure do," Birdie said. It was the way her grandma felt about having a pretty table set, or having flowers on it, or the way some women felt about decorating the house. She just loved to look at beautiful animals.

"So this is Kit, and that's Kat."

"That's cute," Wesley said, looking over at Birdie, and she didn't know what he was thinking, but she was thinking about the nicknames that they'd chosen for each other, Jack and Jill.

"I like that they had matching names, since they'll be pulling as a team in the winter, if I have any business." Becky had done everything right and seemed to be knowledgeable, but she also seemed like she had a good head on her shoulders, knowing that her business might not make it.

Still, it wasn't keeping her from putting everything she had into it, which was indicated by the time spent grooming the horses and making sure they looked beautiful for the ride.

"All right, they're both very calm, and I've ridden them both up and down the beach multiple times, so I don't think you'll have any trouble with them. I would say make sure Kit goes first or else have them side by side. Kat is more of a follower than a leader, and Kit likes to be in front."

"How about you ride Kit then," Birdie said, looking at Wesley, who had admitted that he had some riding experience under his belt.

"All right," he said, going over to the left side of Kit and sticking a foot in the stirrup.

He hopped into the saddle with a graceful ease that Birdie envied. She knew she wouldn't be nearly as smooth and might end up on her rear.

It wasn't as bad as she thought, especially since Kat stood still, not moving at all when Birdie landed a little bit hard in the saddle.

"She really is sweet," Birdie said, thinking that maybe she would be okay, if her horse was this calm.

"I'd trust a child on her, although no horse is bombproof. Any horse could go crazy at any time, just some horses are more likely than others. Kit and Kat are at the low end of the spectrum. Maybe a zero on a scale of 1 to 10."

They laughed, nudged their horses the way Becky had instructed, and Kit went first, while Kat fell in behind.

Sixteen

There was a trail down to the beach that Becky had pointed out to them, and the horses seemed to know it well, since hers went without any instruction from Birdie. There was a certain rhythm to the horse's stride that, once she got used to it, was kind of soothing and easy to fall into.

It was neat to view the world from a slightly different position, and the slow pace made it so that she had time to see everything.

She hadn't realized, even since she'd come to Raspberry Ridge, how frantic the pace of her life had been. Just sitting on the horse's back, moving at a slow walk, forced her to slow down and pay attention to her surroundings. It was the ultimate in relaxation. That, along with the blue sky with big white puffy clouds and a gentle lake breeze that bent the grass around her and made a soothing swishing sound, made her feel like she had almost entered another world. Or at least another dimension.

"I'd forgotten how enjoyable this is." Wesley spoke as they reached the bottom of the trail which ended on the beach. He guided Kit to the side so Kat could come up beside her. "I guess when I was younger though, the big deal about riding horses was making them go fast."

"I don't think that would be nearly as relaxing," Birdie said, her voice having an almost sleepy quality she recognized instantly.

"You're not falling asleep on me, are you?" Wesley said with a laugh.

"I kind of feel like I could. This is...a lot nicer than I thought it was going to be. Although maybe I'm just being lulled into a false sense of security and my horse is going to erupt underneath me any second."

"I would think falling on the sand wouldn't be nearly as bad as falling on...something else."

She didn't think so either. Although she didn't want to fall at all. "I didn't realize Becky wasn't going to go with us."

"I think she needs another horse. Or maybe she just thought that we were mature enough to handle it."

"I don't know. Maybe if we want someone to guide us, we have to say so."

"Her business is new, and she's young. I think she'll settle into what she needs to do."

"You know, I was thinking that if we allowed her to take pictures of our faces, it might help her business." Birdie looked at the ground between her horse's ears. She didn't want to glance at Wesley to see what he was thinking.

She didn't really want to do it, but she wasn't against using her fame to help others, and there was something that Becky stirred in her heart. Something about a scrappy girl who was out in the world trying to make a living, not sitting around on her duff complaining because things weren't good enough, or easy enough, or nothing was handed to her.

"That same thought crossed my mind, but I wasn't going to suggest it to you, because for some reason, I'm thinking you have more to lose than I do."

"I wonder why you have that idea?"

"I don't know. You just seem a little bit more protective of your identity. I want to lie low, but the world's not going to come to an end if I get found out. You, on the other hand, I feel like...it'll be a bigger deal for you."

"I guess it would be. But mostly because people just like to take pictures of me. If they take pictures of you and me together, all of a sudden, I'd have a boyfriend, and we'd be plastered together, and people would be asking you questions like how soon are you going to propose?"

"Do you want me to?" he asked, grinning.

"No. Don't even. You don't know me, you can't possibly be thinking about any kind of long-term relationship."

"Why not? I like you well enough. You're funny, you're cute, and I bet you'd even bounce if you fell off a horse. We could try that out."

"No," she said, grabbing a hold of her horse's mane which is what Becky had told her to do, rather than pulling back on the reins.

"You can also hold on to this. What did she call it, a...pommel?" he asked.

"That's what it was." She wrapped her hand around it, interested to find that it felt kind of good in her hand. Like it was made to grip. Although Becky had told her that it was more for wrapping a rope around.

"She picked the perfect time," Wesley murmured as he looked at the sky that was just starting to turn pink.

"We'll have a great view the whole way there and the whole way back, since it's the western sky, and we're traveling north."

"I thought women weren't supposed to be good with directions."

"Wow. What a misogynistic comment."

He held one hand up. "I was kidding."

"It's a beautiful sky. And you're right. Becky definitely has that down pat. But I think she's a romantic at heart."

"I don't know. She seems a little crusty. Not in that old lady kind of way just in... She has a shell that she doesn't let very many people get past."

"That's pretty astute. I agree with you. What was your degree in? Psychology?"

"I never finished it. I—" He slammed his mouth closed, like he'd done a couple of times before.

Before she could tease him about it, he said, "There was a girl in college. She reminded me of you, and in fact I thought maybe you were her there for a little bit. She helped me with my English composition class. Which is the only way I passed it." He held his hand up again and hurried on. "I never cheated. She never wrote anything for me, but she looked at the things I did write and gave me ideas for improvement."

"That sounds nice," Birdie said, thinking that there was probably more to the story, because it didn't seem like he was stopping.

"We decided that we could pretend to be a couple. I was kind of popular on campus, and she was studious but nerdy. So, she helped me with my paper, and being seen together with me, as we pretended to be together, helped her get a little more popular, and she ended up being class president our senior year. Only I was out of there by then."

"Well. A fake...relationship." She had never done any such thing, although she'd heard of people doing them. Pretending to be together to fool the paparazzi, if they were a big star, or if someone's parents were pushing them to have a significant other, either for a wedding or just because it was that time of their life.

"Didn't you find lying difficult?"

"We never really lied. We just hung out together, and I suppose I might have dropped the word 'girlfriend' around some."

Wild. That he was so...popular on campus that he could just drop the word "girlfriend" and she went from wallflower to class president.

"You have some pretty big star power," she said, thinking that maybe she had misjudged him. He was so goofy and funny that she never really thought about him being well known and popular, but he obviously was. Somewhere. Doing something.

"I didn't really have any other serious girlfriends, not that she was serious, but I was busy...doing other things," he ended with a grin, and she had to return his smile.

"You almost did it again."

"I know. I seem to have more trouble with that than you do. Which again leads me to the fact that I think you might have more at stake than I do."

"I don't know. Maybe." She didn't really want to get into it, because she might end up telling him more than what she wanted to. She trusted him, and that had a tendency to make her mouth a little bit looser.

"So what about you? Aren't you gonna tell me about some kind of weird relationship in your past?"

"No. I don't have any fake engagements in my past. I just have...men that I thought wanted me for me, but I found out they just wanted me for my money. I suppose they wanted me for other things too, but men, you know?"

"Was that a slam against my gender? And if it was, was I included?" He looked over at her, partially joking, but there was a pity in his eyes that made her back feel itchy. She didn't want people's pity.

"It was just a fact. Isn't that true?"

"That men want money? Or that men want sex?"

"I didn't say the S word."

"You didn't have to. I knew what you meant. I was a little offended, because I'm pretty sure that you've spent a lot of time with me and I've never asked you for either."

"No. You're right. You haven't. That's probably why I'm talking to you about it."

"What do you mean?"

"I guess I have trust issues. And for good reason. Actually for five good reasons."

He huffed out a breath. "So it's five guys that have done the give me money, give me sex or I'm leaving you routine?"

"That's kind of a crude way to put it."

"I was just paraphrasing you."

She had done things she wished she wouldn't have. Things that seemed like everyone else was doing and it didn't bother them at all. So why did it bother her so much?

"Maybe that's why I have Gram with me. It's not that I can't control myself, and it's not that I get wrapped up in things and go crazy. It's just... I want to remind myself of what's important to me. And I don't want to get talked into something I know I don't want."

"A no-strings-attached relationship?"

"Exactly."

"The only kind of relationship that two people who don't even know each other's real names could have."

"Yeah."

"So you were warning me," he said, like he had just figured it out, and his eyes went up to the sky, which was slowly turning pink and orange above the lake.

"Not really. I told you. I trust you."

"You trust me enough to tell me that you don't trust me."

That really wasn't what she meant. She hadn't meant to say any of that. But he knew more about her past relationships than she told anyone, although she'd gone through them in the sight of the entire world. The world just didn't know her side of it. Since any time they broke up, it had been the man who had gone on to tell all, and she had holed up, nursing her stupid broken heart.

She didn't want to do that again.

"So no relationship unless there's marriage involved?"

"I've sworn off men completely. I don't want a relationship at all. I don't have time for it, and I haven't found them to be especially beneficial to me. But I have found them to be expensive."

"So how about any man who wants to be in a relationship with you needs to sign a prenup."

She hadn't thought of that. "I kind of feel like they'd find a way around it."

"You must be worth a lot, if it's worth their time to try to find their way around a prenup."

She didn't say anything. She didn't really need to. He'd hit the nail right on the head. The thing was, she knew he wasn't a scammer, and he wasn't after her money either, because he didn't even know that she had any. And as far as she could tell, he didn't know who she was. There was a part of her that said she could trust him, and he could possibly be an exception to her no-relationship rule, since if he liked her, which he had said he did, it wasn't because of her money or her fame. Or what she could do for his career. Although... She still didn't know what that was.

Seventeen

Birdie wanted to stop thinking about her past. Since about guy number two, she'd been hyper concerned, and she still managed to get burned three more times. The last time by a guy who had been recommended by her agent, of all people. She thought she could trust him, because of the recommendation, but she'd been dead wrong.

He sighed and looked off in the distance. "I didn't realize there were going to be this many obstacles. And I don't think you're having fun. Not like we had before."

He seemed sad about it. But he was right. Why couldn't she just let go and continue to trust him, the way she had?

Except trusting people hadn't done her any favors.

"I'm sorry. I... I guess I like you. And I'm telling myself all the reasons why I shouldn't, and they really have nothing to do with you. Nothing to do with anything that you've done, and—"

"And it's not fair to me."

"Life's not fair. I'm just trying to do the best thing for myself. I'm here to rest, relax, to destress. Not to have the stress of a new relationship, and then the worry of what's going to happen to it, and then the inevitable breakup."

"I don't think there's going to be an inevitable breakup with me. I...

I don't intend to have multiple relationships. I've always thought that was a bad idea. It doesn't teach you anything except to leave when things get hard."

She didn't say anything for a while, thinking about that radical new idea. But it didn't take her long to see the parallels. When a person found someone they liked, they were free to go after them, enjoy the feelings, develop a relationship, and then things got hard and they broke up. Over and over and over again.

Because it was easier to find someone else when they had all those new happy feelings than it was to actually work through the problems and stay with the same old, boring person.

"Why does the rest of the world not see that?" she said on a dry laugh that held no humor.

"I thought I was kinda radical. I think that's what you were saying."

"Jack, you're radical."

"Best compliment I've ever been given by a woman," he said, but then he laughed in the silence, and she realized that she probably had been a wet blanket their entire ride. And she didn't mean to be that either. Wes didn't deserve it. There were a lot of other guys that she'd been with who had, but not Wes. He'd gone out of his way to make her laugh and make sure that she was enjoying herself. He'd also gamely watched six children that morning, just because her grandmother signed him up.

"There isn't a single other person I've ever dated who would have watched six kids just because my grandma wanted him to."

"I told you, I thought it was a good thing. Another ten years or so, and I might want to do it again."

"I have to tell Gram not to sign you up for that next time. You'd rather scrub toilets."

"Give me my brush, Jill. Amen. I mean, not literally."

"Well, with toilets, one never knows."

She wasn't sure how far along the beach they'd gone, but it felt like a long way. And the sky was ablaze with color. Soon it would start to fade, and darkness would descend.

"I'm not sure I can get my horse turned around," Birdie said.

"I was thinking about dismounting for a minute. The sky is pretty, the beach has widened out a little bit, and it's a pretty spot."

He was right, the beach had narrowed there for a while and was barely wide enough for the two horses to walk abreast. It was swampy along the edge, and it just looked a lot different than where they were down in Raspberry Ridge.

"We should have gone south. We'd have seen that lighthouse."

"I'm pretty sure there's someone living in it."

"How do you know?"

"I saw some kids running around playing, and a couple, they didn't look like a young couple, but they didn't look exceptionally old either, holding hands while they watched them. It was...a nice family evening, and just watching them made me feel peaceful and hopeful."

She wanted a life like that, a family like that, a peaceful time like that. She got the feeling that he admired that too.

Of course, in order to have that, she'd have to trust someone. Have a relationship.

"I'd like to stop here for a minute and get out of the saddle. If that's all right with you."

"Sure. Um. If I get out, will you help me back in?"

"Sure. Although, I thought maybe a walk would stretch my legs a bit."

She laughed. "I think I am detecting some sports vibes here, since I'm perfectly content to sit on my big animal and allow it to carry me wherever it wants to."

"We can be different but still get along," he quipped, shooting her a grin but training his eyes on the horizon as she held the reins in one hand and walked so that she was beside him.

"When I was a kid, I used to wonder what was on the other side of the setting sun." She wasn't sure what prompted her to say that; it was a dumb idea. And of course as soon as she was old enough to know better, she knew that it was just outer space.

"It's kind of a romantic idea. Beyond the setting sun," he said.

"Sporty and romantic. You must be a movie star."

"No. I would never last in Hollywood."

She wanted to ask why, but the sky was pretty, reflected off the lake, and he was right, it was romantic. Not just beyond the setting sun, but standing in front of it.

"If you could have anything, anything at all, right now. What would you want?" he asked.

It was usually the woman who asked questions like that, and she smiled a little to herself, but it was sweet that his romantic side was coming out, or maybe he really wanted to know. She tried to give it serious thought.

"I don't know. I guess I'm tempted to say I'd like for everyone to be happy, including me, but I know that stuff can happen, and it seems kind of lame. Like I should want something amazing, but all I really want is to be part of a family, with my gram, with God at the center, you know? After yesterday, I'm not sure I want kids, but maybe if I can specifically request nice kids, who don't pee their pants and who stop running once in a while to actually carry on a conversation."

"I don't think all kids are like that. Those guys just had a rough start and need somebody who's willing to take on such a huge task and see what they can do with them."

"Yeah. What about you? What would you want if you could have anything?"

"I want the same thing. A family for Gramps and me. One with God at the center, like you said. Because that's the only thing that can bring peace to the crazy."

There was that word again. Peace. That was a word that seemed to recur every time she started writing for her new album. It was the feeling she got now as she thought about looking beyond the setting sun. Looking forward to tomorrow, to next week, to next year. Did she really want to continue down the path of pop superstar? Is that what she wanted for the rest of her life?

That wouldn't give her peace.

A gentle breeze flowed across the lake, and Birdie wasn't sure whether it was because of the breeze, or because of what she was thinking, but her fingers touched his.

She didn't pull away, and neither did he. In fact, she turned toward him, curling her fingers around his as she did so and linking them together.

His brow twitched. He got a questioning look on his face and then looked at their hands.

"I didn't do that," he said.

She snorted. Of course he was going to make a joke. He could always make her laugh.

"Is it okay?" she asked.

The reason she asked was because he had said that he wasn't going to go from relationship to relationship and he said he hadn't done that. And...here she was, not exactly dragging him into a relationship, holding someone's hand didn't exactly mean that they were committed for the next hundred years, but she assumed it was something he hadn't done a whole lot.

"That's a good question," he said, and she got the feeling that he was stalling. "I like it. I want to keep doing it, but I'm not the kind of guy that has a summer fling and then walks away from it. We just talked about that."

For once, he was serious as he looked into her eyes. While he was talking though, he wound their fingers more tightly together, until their palms touched and their hands were clasped.

"Are you demanding a commitment out of me?"

"Not demanding. I asked. I...don't typically go around doing this, and I want to know what your intentions are."

"I think I intend to kiss you." She couldn't believe the words as they came out of her mouth.

Apparently she wasn't the only one, since his brow didn't just quirk, it shot way up.

"Right now?" he asked, and he sounded more than a little panicked.

She tried not to laugh. "Is that gonna be a problem?"

"No?" he said, but he looked at her like it was going to be a problem. He looked a little scared.

"I just wanted to see if you're serious. You could have been feeding me a line of BS back there. All of this, I don't have relationships, and I only do it if it's serious, and all that."

He visibly relaxed. "You were just testing me." He nodded, closing his eyes and then rolling them. "I should have seen that coming."

"No. If you saw it coming...you wouldn't have been real."

His lips pulled back, and his eyes crinkled. "I'm real all right, Jill."

"I'm sorry," she said, feeling guilty as she saw how surprised he was. "I don't believe in playing games, and yet, there I was. Testing you. That might not be a foolish, hurtful game, but still not right." She put her hand on his forearm.

He looked down at it, then brought his other hand up and put his hand on hers, running his thumb over her fingers. "I understand. I'm not agreeing, but I understand that when you've been hurt, you have things that you do to try to keep it from happening again."

"And I suppose that's one of the reasons why you have the policy that you do. No relationships until you're sure it's the right one. That keeps you from having history or baggage like I do."

"Exactly. Although, I have to say, Gramps can be a goofball, but he was the one who taught me that. He and Gram before she died. She was the soul of our home. And she often said that she saw so many of her girlfriends regretful of the relationships that they'd had before they were married, but she and Gramps had never been with anyone else. It was… something I was brought up with."

"By your grandparents. It's so old-fashioned." Although, old-fashioned didn't necessarily mean bad. Sometimes what seemed like "progressive" was actually regressive, and the same old, same old sin that hadn't worked the first time.

She sighed and stared at his shoulder. "How do you know when the right one is standing in front of you?" she asked, wanting with all of her heart to know the answer to that. The pull toward him was so strong, and she wanted to take another step, wanted to put her arms around him and feel him hold her. The temptation was almost more than she could stand.

"I think God will show you. I don't think He's going to demand that you get married to someone you're not attracted to or that you don't like. But He's going to be clear, because it's an important decision. Just sometimes we let our emotions get involved first."

She looked up at him, knowing that her emotions were already involved. She wanted to put a hand around the back of his neck and tug his head down. To feel his lips on hers and to get lost in the moment.

"What if the other person doesn't feel the same?" she asked, trying to keep the edge of fear out of her voice. Maybe that was part of the problem. She always thought that it was just her money and her fame that was going to attract people and no one would actually like her for her.

"Sometimes we have to wait. Sometimes it's just not God's timing. Maybe they'll come around, but maybe we're wrong. Or maybe they're just not going to follow God's leading. Maybe they got caught up in the moment and in their emotions with someone else."

"That's sad. Then they miss out."

"Yeah. On a lifetime of happiness. Lifetime of having the exact one that God wanted for you, which would be the very best thing for you, because God always knows, doesn't He?"

"I know He does. Though sometimes it's hard to believe. Hard to have faith and wait."

"The waiting is the hardest." He took his hand and brushed it lightly over the top of her hair, pushing a strand away from her face and trailing his fingers down it until his hand rested on her shoulder. "I like you. A lot. I...can't stop thinking about kissing you."

She closed her eyes. That is exactly how she felt. She liked him a lot and couldn't stop thinking about having him kiss her.

"At least we're thinking along the same lines," she said, a little humor in her voice, but it was still shaking. She wasn't quite sure why. It felt like an important moment.

The waves rolled in on the beach, making a soothing sound as the gentle breeze lifted a piece of hair and blew it across her face.

He lifted his hand and tucked it back behind her ear.

"We better get going," he said, but he didn't make a move to leave, and neither did she.

One of the horses snorted and stomped on the sand, and maybe that was what finally broke the spell that seemed to be wrapped around them, so they could leave, but they didn't. She wasn't sure she could.

Finally, he took a deep breath and blew it out.

"Come on. It's going to be dark before we get home now." He took another breath as he slowly backed away from her, letting his hands drop to his sides. "You want me to help you mount?"

"I was able to get on by myself at the barn," she said, her voice seeming to come from far away as she tried to rein in her out-of-control emotions and deal with the disappointment. There wasn't going to be a kiss. And she knew that was for the best. She knew his way was better than hers, but it wasn't what she wanted in the moment. Although in the long term, she supposed it would be what she wanted.

It was the idea of skipping dessert in order to stick to a diet. It was hard to do in the short term, but the next day when the scale showed its approval, she would be happy with her choice.

"If you don't mind holding her?" she asked as she turned toward her horse, putting a hand underneath the mane on her silky neck.

"Not at all. If you need me to do something else, I'm totally willing. Just let me know."

"I appreciate it." She swallowed and put her foot in the stirrup.

She stopped when she felt his hand on her shoulder.

"Birdie?"

"Yeah?" she asked, staring at the saddle horn and trying to keep her voice modulated.

"You're mad at me."

"No. I'm frustrated at myself. And disappointed because I wanted to kiss you." She snorted. "That's all."

There. She wasn't usually shy about voicing her opinion, but she didn't typically go around telling men that she wanted to kiss them either. Particularly men she wasn't in a relationship with. She wasn't in anything with Wesley. She wasn't sure what a person could call what they had together.

"I wanted the same. No. I still do."

"Then why not just do it?" she said, turning her head and looking at him, knowing that there was irritation on her face, but unable to contain it. "Why tiptoe around, scared to commit?"

"I wasn't the one scared to commit. That was you. I just told you, when I commit, I'm looking at marriage, I'm not looking at spending some good times together, then going our separate ways."

"Marry?" she asked, not recalling hearing that word in the conversation at all.

Her foot fell out of the stirrup as she turned with her hands on her hips. "You didn't say anything about that." And she wasn't sure whether that would change the conversation or not. Possibly it would have scared her away.

"That's kinda frowned upon in our society. Talking about marriage before I'm even in a relationship with a girl. But that's what I'm looking at. I'm not out for a good time, although there's a part of me that wants that. But most of me wants to find a girl I can build a life with. Not just spend a few hours with, then leave. I want something that's going to last. Like my grandparents. It didn't happen overnight, I know that. And there's a lot of work that goes into a relationship even after a marriage, but I just don't think that the right way to go about it is trying out ten or twenty or more girls, until I think I found the right one, then hope she sticks around long enough for us to date for five years before we talk about getting married."

She swallowed. He didn't exactly sound angry, but he sounded... forceful. Like he didn't expect her to listen to him, let alone agree. But she knew he was right. It was just logical.

"And I asked how you know, know that you are with the right one."

Maybe that was what she was getting at. She wanted to be the right one.

Eighteen

"I told you that you know who your right match is because God shows you." Wesley was silent for a moment, and then he said, "I think God gives us the prerequisite that the person that you're with has to be a believer. The Bible clearly says that we are not to be unequally yoked with unbelievers. We're not to even think about a relationship with them. So, when you go into a relationship, that should be the first question. Are they a believer? That makes sense. But yet, how many Christians do that?"

"We just look for someone that we like, because that's what we've been taught."

"And that's what I'm saying. We've been taught wrong."

She lifted her shoulder and nodded.

"Of course, if we're truly Christians, we'll be attracted to someone else who is a Christian, because non-Christians aren't going to be doing things that attract us, but so many of us are nominal Christians, or Christians in name only, but we have no actual desire to read the Bible or please God."

"You just described pretty much every Christian I know."

He nodded. "Sometimes that's me too, but I don't want to be. I can't say I'm a Christian, and then if a non-believing girl wants me anyway, be okay with that. I have to actively look for girls who are Christians. Because of what the Bible says."

"Because we are not allowed to marry non-Christians."

"Yes. And the world wants to knock that out of us. They want to call us racists or narrow minded, or whatever else they want to call us, but it's just the devil making up names to try to get us to disobey what's in the Bible."

He laughed and looked at the ground. "I guess I get a little passionate about it, because people have made fun of me because I've said that, and it's so radical, so unacceptable in today's society, that a lot of times, people, Christians, haven't even heard of it."

"And yet it's biblical."

"Exactly."

"So any Christian will do?"

"Maybe? God gives us free choice. I do think He will guide us, but I also think that He gave us guidelines, told us that who we choose has to be a Christian and a member of the opposite sex. Those things are clear in scripture. But as for a specific person, He doesn't really say. And love is a choice—we can choose to love and be committed to anyone, whether we're 'in love' with them or not. Although, I do feel like if we ask Him, like I was saying earlier, He will guide us to the right one." He lifted his shoulder. "Maybe more like He'll say this was a good choice, that one's not. I don't know. Maybe He's more specific than that, but I've never felt that way."

"So as long as you have the same values, the same morals, and you feel like you can get along with them, and they're a Christian, living according to the Bible, then it might be okay?"

"Sure. I guess I would say it's also good to get the advice of trusted Christian advisors, your parents if possible. They're the ones who love you. They're the ones who care about you."

"At our age, should we really be asking our parents?"

"Why not? Are they not as smart now as they were when we were kids?"

"It just seems really weird for someone of my age to go and ask, and of course since I don't have parents, it would have to be my gram."

"You think she would give you bad advice?"

"I don't think so. I think she wants me to be happy, and... I guess you're right. It just seems odd."

"That's because society has made it odd, much to the devil's delight. If you have good Christian friends, you could ask them. Friends who know what the Bible says and have experience. But I guess I would be cautious asking someone our own age. You want someone who's been there and done that, at least I do. Someone with experience. Although... Different people probably give you different advice, so it's always best to go back to God and the Bible."

"It just feels really confusing," she said as her horse shifted and she realized that full darkness had fallen.

"We really should go," she said, turning and putting her foot in the saddle stirrup, and managing to get on by holding tight to the pommel and pulling hard.

He waited until she was settled before he handed her the reins and then went around and got on his own horse. He did it so easily, made it look so effortless that it made her even more envious. She was already envious about the way that he lived his life with purpose. It seemed so much smarter than what she had done.

"Gramps thinks you're a pretty good choice," he said, "by the way."

They'd barely taken three steps, and she turned to him, shocked.

"Seriously? You've talked about me?"

"Sure. You're our neighbor. Of course we've talked about you. Although, I'm not sure whether he thinks you're a good choice because of you or because of your gram's cooking and he can just see that there'd be benefits for me being married to you."

"Yes. Everyone wants me for my benefits."

She didn't really mean that. She was mostly teasing. And he didn't say anything more.

The horses were surefooted thankfully, because she couldn't see the ground from where she sat, although she could see the starlight shining off the water and hear the lapping of the waves along the shore.

"I know there are some people who think you have a soulmate, someone who is destined to be with you, and you just have to keep searching the world to find it, but I don't really think I believe that. Since we have a tendency to find our soulmate very close to where we happen to be, and what are the odds that we're going to be living or working next to the one in eight billion who was made for us?"

"Yeah. Although it stands to reason that if God made your soulmate, He would put them close to you, so that you at least ran into them."

"Yeah, Christians can believe that, but people who don't believe in a god are kind of up a creek without a paddle."

"I never understood that saying. Shouldn't it be down a creek without a paddle? Since if you're up a creek, you can just float down?"

"Well, I think originally the creek didn't contain water."

She laughed, realizing that he was probably right. She still felt embarrassed for wanting to kiss him and pushing for it when he didn't want to, but beyond that, things between them hadn't changed. He was still funny and easy to talk to, and she knew she could say pretty much anything and he wouldn't be offended. In fact, she couldn't think of anything that she could try to talk about that he wouldn't take rationally and easily. The way he'd done with everything.

"So what do you think?" he asked. The horses continued to walk in the dark, following the shore of the lake as they went through the narrow part with the marsh on their left.

"About what?" she asked, surprised. She'd been lost in her own thoughts, a jumble of what her future might look like, the things that they had talked about this evening, ways she could implement that in her life, and whether or not she'd ever find a man since she wanted one just like Wesley, and she didn't even know who he was. Men like him were very, very rare.

"About marriage, relationships, us." He said the words slowly, with a pause between each one, like either he hoped to get her to think, or he was dragging his feet about asking, because it made him uncomfortable.

Either one could be true for her.

"I think you're right about relationships, and I think you're right about marriage too. It should be done as closely to the Bible as possible. But I think as long as two people are Christians, they can make it work. So I agree with you on the whole idea of a soulmate. I also am not sure about asking God and getting His confirmation, since He doesn't talk to you in an audible voice. But the idea of getting advice from people who are older and wiser than you makes a lot of sense to me."

She would have a lot to chew on. Because she got a little bit stumbled up with the whole idea of asking God if this was the right person for her versus God giving her free choice and just showing her if it was a good idea or not. She didn't know how any of that worked. But maybe she was making it more complicated than it needed to be.

"And?" he prompted.

She tried to think back. "And what?"

"Us."

"You said there was no us."

"I didn't say that."

"That's what I got out of what we talked about. I told you I wanted to kiss you, and it didn't happen. I assume that's because...you might have wanted it, but it wasn't a good idea."

"I think maybe we get the kissing first and it's out of line. I wanted to see where we might be going with this, so that maybe there would be a kiss tonight after all." He looked a little sheepish as he glanced over at her. The moon had come up, and it lay on its side in the sky, reflecting off the water and glinting off his eyes.

"I see. So you want a commitment from me before you kiss me." That was a little bit of teasing, but his comment had made her feel more lighthearted. Maybe things were not going in the direction that she had thought after all. Or hadn't hit the dead end it felt like.

"It doesn't have to be a one-hundred-year commitment where you can't break off if you change your mind, but I want to know that you're looking for someone the same as I am and you think that I might be him. I guess...I need that much."

"I'd like even more."

"What do you want?" he asked, surprised.

"Well, if that's all it takes, just a knowledge that you're both Christians, that you have the same values and morals and you kind of like each other, then you should have rings and vows before a kiss." She was saying it kind of lightly, and she wasn't sure she agreed with that, but it made sense if they took the direction their conversation was going out to the bitter end.

"So I need to get a ring."

"Do you?" she asked, and she thought maybe she was being coy when she didn't really mean to be.

"The more time I spend with you, the more I don't want to spend time with anyone else. But I kinda saw you as someone who would be leaving my circle and never coming back. I kept cautioning myself that it might not be a good idea. But if that's not true. If you're willing to be committed to me, we'll figure it out. It might be hard. I don't know. Since I don't know what you do."

"And I don't know what you do."

"So we'll have to work that all out, but... You don't seem to be unreasonable, and some people have said that I am, but I try not to be."

"People say you're unreasonable?" She didn't mean to interrupt him, but that surprised her.

"I'm known as being fairly aggressive at my...what I do. Maybe it's a reputation that got made for itself, and I had to step into it. Regardless, yeah. But that's not who I want to be."

"Sometimes what we want to be and what we are are two very different, very not similar things at all."

"True. Sometimes we deceive ourselves. We're good liars."

"Especially to ourselves," she said, having to agree with him, but her heart was beating fast, and her mind was running over what he had said. He was willing to give her a ring. Like, an engagement ring. Like, this could be a serious relationship.

Now that the drive to kiss him had faded, and she was thinking rationally... She still liked him. Still thought that there was no man better. That he was one in a million or maybe even one in a billion. She couldn't imagine there being a whole lot of men like Wesley walking the earth, and he wanted her.

But more than that, she wanted him. She didn't want to be with someone who only wanted her for publicity or money. And the man had admitted that he wasn't sure what she did for a living. So he must not recognize her. Which meant he didn't really know what he was getting when he got her. All the stuff that came with her.

"Do you think you might change your mind if you find out that there are a lot of things that come with me? I'm not talking material things. I'm talking stress and frustration and scheduling conflicts and things that are time-consuming and difficult." She didn't know how to explain the amount of time that she usually put into her business. How exhausting it was to travel the globe and put on huge shows night after night. How hands-on she was with everything that happened in her business and making sure that things went the way she wanted them to.

"You have to keep it?"

"Whoa." Her horse stopped. That wasn't what she meant, and she laughed. "How do I get it to go again?"

"I assume you didn't want to make your horse stop?" he said as he pulled gently back on the reins and his stopped as well, and he looked over his shoulder at her.

She remembered what Becky had said and nudged her horse forward.

They started again, and she went back to thinking about what he had just asked her.

"Are you one of those chauvinists who think that a woman should be barefoot and pregnant in the kitchen all the time?" she asked, trying not to offend him but realizing that she was slightly offended herself.

"I think a household is happier if they do things the way God intended, and God definitely said that women were supposed to take care of the house and the kids. The man was supposed to protect and provide. I was just asking a question though. I wasn't trying to get your shoes off or anything."

She laughed at the way he said "or anything," which implied everything else that she had said.

"Good. Because I'm keeping my shoes on for now. And I'm definitely going to buy a pair of boots the next time if I can find any place that sells them."

She couldn't believe she didn't have a pair of riding boots in her wardrobe. She had sparkly boots and fancy boots and dress boots, but she didn't have a pair of riding boots. Ones that she could put on and wouldn't look totally out of place when she was on the back of a horse.

"All right. Not trying to keep you out of your boots," he said.

There was laughter in his voice, but she knew his statement had been serious.

There wasn't really a way she could argue with that. What was she supposed to say, "Maybe God didn't know what He was talking about?"

She could say that the men who wrote the Old Testament had provincial views and modern society had evolved beyond those views, but it would be easy for him to say that God could have had the Bible written at any point in history. Because He's God and He chose when it would be written and by whom. But He'd had it written at that point, and he could have had anything included or not included in it, and God chose to include the fact that women had a place in the home, jobs they were supposed to do, things that were solely on their shoulders to keep the world running smoothly.

"I guess you're right. I don't like it, but I don't have any arguments for it."

"That's kind of the way the Bible is sometimes, isn't it? We don't always like it, but you can't argue. Unless you want to say you know better than God," he said, his shoulders moving up in the semi-darkness. "I've had more than one discussion with Him, and I just had to humble myself and tell Him that I was wrong."

"Well, it's nice to know that I'm not the only one."

They walked on, and Birdie thought she saw the lights of Raspberry Ridge not far ahead in the distance on the left. She was a little sad that their time together was growing short, but she was starting to get chilly, since she hadn't brought a jacket, and it had cooled off considerably once the sun went down.

"So... Maybe we want to think about things?" Wesley broke the silence between them.

"Yeah. I suppose if I'm not ready to be a full-time wife and mom, or at least wife, I probably should just keep focusing on my career." The thought made her sad. And the idea of having children... Even though they had just watched children that were really difficult, she still wanted children of her own.

"So how long do you think you're going to be around?" he asked. "If that's not too pressing. I'm not trying to ask you questions that you can't answer."

"I appreciate the consideration. Although, I don't mind being asked questions that make me think. You know how sometimes your answers change?"

"Yeah. That happens to me all the time. Sometimes my answer might have been different last week, but I was a different person last week, you know? So facts don't change, but answers that are based on feelings and what we want absolutely can."

"I agree."

That seemed to close out what they had been talking about before, and then she thought about his next question. "I wasn't really trying to put you off with the next question. I just wanted to make sure you understood that I'm not sure how I feel, and maybe that'll change. Anyway, I can't stay past September. I have things that are happening and a path I'm going down that I can't get out of."

"I see. I guess I'm the same. September happens to be my cutoff too. Maybe about the last Friday or so, I'll have to leave."

"Really?"

He was leaving. Why hadn't that occurred to her? It wasn't like this was something that would last forever.

"I don't like to think about end dates."

"We all have them. They happen."

So true. Everyone died. She didn't know why she hated them and got sad thinking about them. So she just didn't, then was surprised to realize that her time here wasn't just an isolated bubble that floated on endlessly.

She loved what they had done so far, just hanging out in the afternoon, helping each other write, doing fun things, eating supper together, feeling like family. Seeing her gram and his gramps laugh and joke together. Seeing her gram throw herself into everything here and get active and involved the way she loved. She hated the idea that that wasn't going to be her life forever, but that she had to go back, traveling from city to city, doing tours and shows and meeting with executives and making decisions about her business.

It felt so heavy and stressful and no wonder she needed to take a break. Except, it felt like she hardly got started, and now she was thinking about the end.

"You got quiet again. I guess that means you're thinking."

"Yeah. You asked me a question that definitely got my brain working. I love what I do. I feel very blessed to be able to do what I do. There are so many people who would love to be able to make a living the way I do, but... It's gotten to be a lot. And I wonder if I'll ever be happy going back to just a little? Something manageable. Or do I have to give it all up?"

"I guess I could talk to you about it if you want to, but I might not be the best person, because I have a tendency to run full steam ahead."

He didn't seem like that here, but she could kinda see that in him. Where he was driven to be the best, and he worked hard. He certainly didn't shrink from any opportunities or any work here. After all, he gamely watched four wild children and a set of twins. She didn't know any other man in the world who would do that, so he had to be in the top one percent of whatever it was that he did.

"I think the path is here," he said, pointing through the sand toward the barn.

She had no idea how he saw anything, but she said, "All right. I'll follow you." Assuming that if they got lost, they wouldn't be lost for long. Plus, they were on horses, surely they could cover more ground that way. Although, whether that would actually help if they truly got lost or not, she wasn't sure.

"Bingo. This is it. I see our tracks from earlier and recognize the formation of those three bushes."

"I'm glad you were paying attention. I wasn't at all."

"I was having a great time, but I also wanted to make it back. I... don't want to get you lost or lose you."

"Well, I've been with you the whole time." She laughed. "And so far, it's always been fun."

"It could change at any time," he said, and she thought he was mostly joking. "But I had a great time. Would you be interested in doing it again tomorrow evening? Making it a regular thing?"

"I'd love it," she said, not needing to think about her schedule and loving that. That was one of the nice things about not having all the pressure of the tour and her business and all the things she had to direct on her. She didn't have to think about what she was doing tomorrow. She made her own plans. And she really, really enjoyed that.

Although, she wasn't so naïve as to think that if she quit touring, and backed out of being a pop singer, that she could actually have a regular life, and that would include being able to plan whatever she wanted whenever she wanted. That just wasn't possible. There were going to have to be concessions. No life was perfect.

The barn came into view, and they saw Becky sitting on the top of a fence board, staring down at the ground between her feet.

"I bet you thought we were lost," Wesley said as they rode up.

She hopped off as soon as she heard his voice and turned toward them, the light from the barn shining on her face. She was smiling and didn't look the slightest bit worried.

"I figured you'd be back eventually. Although, it's easy to miss the trail down to the lake, and I thought you might end up coming through town."

"We could have gone up the bluffs path. It's not that steep," Wesley agreed.

"But Wesley was able to find it easily. I would have totally missed it, and I'm not sure I would have thought about going up the bluffs right away. I probably would have spent a lot of time looking for the path and panicking." She was just being honest, and she appreciated the fact that Wesley was there. He helped her, and she was going to give him credit for it.

"All right, how do you like it? Did the mares do well for you?"

"They did great."

"So well, in fact, we'd like to come back tomorrow, if that's okay?"

"That would be awesome. What time?"

"Same time?"

"Well, I don't have anyone else booked, so that'll be fantastic," Becky said, looking like she was indeed pretty happy.

"You don't have to sit around and wait on us though," Wesley said as they dismounted.

"I didn't. I actually was working on the fence until it got dark, and then I hit my thumb with a hammer and decided that I better wait until morning and the sun comes out and gives me a little bit of light before I keep going."

She laughed, like hitting herself with a hammer wasn't that big of a deal, but it made Birdie's stomach clench. Ouch.

"I didn't hear you yelling, so that is impressive," Wesley joked as he handed the reins of his horse to Becky and went around to touch

Birdie's waist as she dismounted. She appreciated his steadying hand and felt that if she had a little bit more practice, maybe she wouldn't be quite so awkward at the whole thing.

"You know, that's just part of farming. You get something that hurts almost every day, although some days are worse than others," Becky said.

That was probably true. Even in her line of work, she got hurt at times. But as a farmer, someone working with large animals and equipment day in and day out, the odds were good that something was going to happen, even if it was something little.

They set up a time for the next day and then walked out to the car. They got into it without saying anything, and Birdie finally broke the silence as they pulled out on Main Street in Raspberry Ridge.

"Thank you. I really, really appreciate you going. I could have done it by myself, but it wouldn't have been nearly as fun."

"I wouldn't have wanted to do it by myself. I still don't. The only reason I enjoy horseback riding is because you're with me."

"We don't have to do it if you don't want to!" she said, immediately feeling bad that she was pushing her dreams on him, and he had sacrificed in order to make her happy.

"No. I love that we have a reoccurring time set up. Actually two of them, if you count the afternoon at one o'clock on the beach and then evenings at seven. Two times a day I get to look forward to seeing you."

"Still, we really don't have to do this. We could see each other doing something else? What would you like?"

"Nothing. It's perfect. And I do enjoy horseback riding. It's just... I wouldn't enjoy it without you."

She wasn't sure exactly what he was saying. Maybe she was reading too much into it, but he had given her the idea that he did want to have a relationship, he just didn't want to have one that wasn't meaningful. Or going somewhere. That didn't have a purpose. And she wasn't sure that she could promise him that. She had to think about it. Actually, she knew in her heart that she wanted to and she hoped that she could, but maybe the idea was just so big, so different than what she'd always thought all of her life, that she just needed time to get used to it.

Twenty

Wesley felt like a million bucks as they pulled into Birdie's house. He'd had the best time with her. Except... Some of the glow dimmed as he realized that she really hadn't given him an answer, and this might be leading to disaster. He didn't want it to, but he'd always been careful to make sure he didn't allow himself to get into a deep relationship where there was going to be pain at the end.

He thought again of the girl that he had a fake relationship with in college.

Was there something wrong with him? Was there something that was broken inside of him that he was afraid to have relationships? He thought he was doing what the Bible said, what God wanted him to do, but it was so different than what everyone else did, and while he didn't doubt himself very often, he found himself wondering now. Was he doing the right thing?

He couldn't answer that with a straight yes, and it concerned him.

Usually he could.

Maybe he just needed to get back in the Bible and remind himself of what was important. Not allowing himself to be emotionally entangled with people who didn't actually want to have serious relationships, and not being with anyone unless they were thinking of marriage... It was crazy, but he found those principles in the Bible far more than he could find any justification for dating. And it just seemed wise to not give away little pieces of his heart to every girl that came along. But to protect it for the one girl that he was going to spend his lifetime with.

He wanted a whole heart to give her. Something pure and beautiful. Something that he could give without regrets or thoughts of anyone else.

Maybe his idea was too perfect. Like a socialist utopia that sounded good on paper but was impossible with a world steeped in sin and selfishness. After all, who wanted to give up stuff that they'd worked for in order to help people who didn't work eat? Jamestown had been a miserable failure when they tried that, and he didn't see it ever working, except possibly among a group of pure Christians, maybe like the early church in Acts, but even he didn't know any modern Christians who were dedicated enough to actually pull that off.

"There's something on your steps," he said as they pulled into the cottages. He always pulled into hers first when he had her with him. Even though it wasn't that far of a walk from his cottage to hers. He just believed that it was best to drop the girl off. To get out and walk her to her door. To make sure that she got in okay. He wasn't going to change that now, even though they were so close together it was almost pointless.

"I see it. Actually, is that a person?"

"It's your grandma!" he said, wanting to accelerate the car, to get there faster, but it was almost time to stop, and it was silly. He checked himself just in time and eased into the spot. But he was out of the car almost the instant he had it in park.

"Gram?"

"Goodness. I thought I was going to have to sit here until midnight."

"What are you doing?" Birdie came over, kneeling down beside Gram who was half sitting, half reclining on the ground in front of the steps.

"There's a meteor shower, and I'm watching for shooting stars."

"Really?" Wesley looked around. He hadn't noticed any shooting stars while he had been on his ride with Birdie, but well, all the shooting stars that he'd seen had been in his head for those few seconds he'd almost kissed her.

"Gram? What meteor shower? What are you talking about? Are you okay?"

"What's your name?" Wesley asked, kneeling down at Gram's head, since there wasn't enough room to get to her other side. She seemed to be propped on the steps a little.

"It's Polly," Gram said, "and no. I broke my leg. I'm lying here because I tried getting up and the pain was just too much."

"You broke your leg, and you're joking about meteor showers?" Birdie said. "And you think I was a difficult child."

"You were a difficult child. I'm just trying to lighten the moment."

"We'll lighten the moment after we get you taken care of."

"Should I call 911?"

"I think around here it would be just as quick to get her in the car and take her to the hospital ourselves, unless we can't, or if she needs a stretcher."

"I don't need a stretcher. If you guys can help me get up, I can get myself to the car, and you can take me on in to the hospital."

"Why didn't you call Gramps?"

"I left my stupid phone in the house. I yelled, but I bet he has his hearing aids out. It's past his bedtime."

"He probably does. I'll text him later and let him know what we've done, unless you don't want me to go?" Wesley stopped, thinking that maybe he was making a lot of assumptions that he shouldn't be making.

"No. Please. If we can get her in the car, I'm not sure I can get her out on my own, although there'll probably be staff there... I'd really like to have you."

"Sure. Let me get the car as close as I can, and then we'll worry about getting her up, okay?"

"I've got stuff in the oven. And you need to turn it off. It's probably burning by now," he heard Gram saying as he walked away to the car.

"Gram, what am I going to do with you?" Birdie said, although as he sat down in the car, he saw her reluctantly get up and run up the stairs and into the cottage.

She was right back out just a moment later, and he saw that she grabbed a blanket and her purse.

He figured that probably had something to do with either getting her warm or getting her in the car, but he wasn't sure which one.

Gram probably needed both.

"We need to watch she doesn't go into shock," he said as he walked over and met her at Gram's side.

They knelt down together.

"I thought the blanket might help us get her in the car, but I can grab another one and we can put it over top of her once we get her in."

"Sounds good to me."

"Gram, we're going to put this underneath you, and we're going to try to lift you up. Okay?" Birdie said, leaning over her grandma as she did so.

"That's fine. I can lift myself up. It's the lower part of my leg that's broken," she said, proving that by putting her hands underneath her and her good foot on the ground and pushing herself up.

She did it so quickly that it took Wesley a moment to realize he was supposed to be moving with the blanket.

He knew that Gramps was rather infatuated with Gram, but he thought that the man might have some difficulty keeping up to her. She was definitely a lady who didn't sit around much.

"Can you pull it down a little on that side," he said as he got it around behind her back, but it needed to be pulled down underneath the rear. Birdie was the better person to do that.

"I got it. I want to make sure I have enough left on this end, without getting too much underneath." She muttered those words as she worked on getting the blanket straightened out and pulled out underneath Gram's thighs.

"I'm glad you don't weigh a thousand pounds, Gram," Birdie said softly.

"I don't know how she doesn't with all the baked goods she's constantly making. I'd definitely weigh that much if I could cook like her."

"Me too."

"Would you stop talking about my weight? Women are kind of sensitive about that subject, in case you didn't know."

"And she's still just as cantankerous as ever," Birdie murmured, looking at him, like they were having a private conversation without her.

"I'm right here," Gram said, and Wesley figured that was coming.

"I see you, Gram. Now, if you can move yourself just a little bit to the side, so I can get on the other side, I think we can pick you up with this blanket."

"All right," Gram said, and she did try to move herself, succeeding in getting a few inches to the side, and then she said, "Ouch!"

"What's the matter?" Birdie said immediately.

Wesley figured she probably bumped her leg somehow, but he didn't say that. If it made Birdie feel better to ask her what was wrong, he'd listen.

"I bumped my leg."

"How did you do this? Fall down the steps?"

"No. I forgot to turn the light on, and instead of going back in and flipping it on, I figured I could just keep going. I wanted to take that trash to the garbage can. Anyway, I forgot that there were four steps instead of three, and after the third step, I started to walk, and the ground was a little further away than what I expected."

"But you are right next to the steps," Birdie said as they adjusted the blanket between them, each of them getting a firm grip. Wesley thought that he could probably pick her up in his arms, but he thought the blanket might be a good thing to have underneath her if they needed to slide her over the back seat of the car.

"I moved myself over there. No one else was coming to save me, and I figured you guys might be out 'til midnight on your date."

"It was not a date," Birdie said immediately.

"Okay. Whatever. He came, he picked you up, he took you somewhere, and I assume he paid."

"I did pay. But I wanted to."

"Just because you want to doesn't make it not a date. In fact, I think that makes it even more of a date."

He hadn't thought about things like that. But they didn't talk about that anymore. "Are you ready?"

"Yes. Once we have her up, I might need to adjust, and if I do, I'll just say 'down.'"

"All right. If you say 'down,' I will try to match my side with yours."

"You guys are making me nervous. Have you done this before? I feel like a guinea pig."

"Gram. You are a guinea pig."

"Well, maybe you should practice on someone else. Is Gramps asleep?"

"We need to get you to the ER. As spry as you are, you could still end up dealing with some shock, and we don't want that. Not here."

"On three?" he said.

"Yeah."

"One, two, three!" They both picked up at the same time, gently elevating her until she was far enough off the ground that they didn't think her leg would get bumped.

"All right. We're going to walk as smoothly as we can to the car." It was just a few feet away, but he knew that any jarring would hurt her leg, no matter how it was broken.

"All right. That hurts," Gram said as they took a step.

"Maybe we should have checked to see if she had any back injuries."

"I told you I moved myself. I don't have back injuries. It's just my leg!"

"I think we would have run into some opposition if we would have tried to do that," Wesley said reasonably.

Birdie must have thought so too, because she didn't argue anymore.

He really wanted to grab the blanket and not have Birdie working so hard, but he resisted the urge, and not just because he thought she would be offended. But he really did think it would be better for Gram to be in the car with the blanket under her butt, in case they needed to move her. It would hopefully be less jostling to her leg.

He ended up having to put his arm behind her back and underneath her anyway, but he was able to grab the blanket and move her as he reached in and slid her.

He could tell that Gram had her teeth clenched and was trying hard not to cry out.

"I'm gonna go around behind you and slide you the rest of the way in."

She nodded but didn't say anything.

He met Birdie's eyes as he stood, and he hated the pain and concern he saw there. He was doing his best, but he wasn't going to be able to keep her from not feeling this.

He found himself wanting to protect Birdie from anything that might cause her pain.

He couldn't remember ever feeling something that strong before, but he tried to tamp the idea down and just focus on what he needed to do as he opened the back door on the opposite side of the car and grabbed the blanket.

"Hold your leg up," he said to Gram, low in her ear and as gently as he possibly could.

"I got it up," she said.

He took a breath and then gripped the blanket in both hands and tugged slowly and steadily.

To his relief, the blankets slid easily on his leather seats, and the old lady's rear came over to the other side.

"I don't think it's going to be comfortable in any way to sit there, with your leg on the seat, and you're going to get tired holding it up. Is there anything that you can think of that would make it feel better?"

"Maybe if Birdie sat back here with me and held it up?" Gram said, sticking her other foot on the floor and keeping her broken leg in the air.

Wesley guessed, if it was broken indeed, it was just a fracture, possibly a hairline one at that. But he didn't doubt the pain. If they were very blessed, maybe she only sprained her ankle. But they wouldn't know until they got to the hospital and had X-rays.

"I'll do it," Birdie said. "Is there anything that anyone needs before I get in?"

She looked at Gram, and Wesley assumed that was who she was talking to.

He took a moment to send a quick text off to Gramps, to let him know where he was going to be for the next few hours.

In his experience, hospitals didn't typically send a person home with a cast on, but it probably depended on who was on duty and what kind of break it was.

After he sent the text, he got in the driver's seat and waited just a few moments until Birdie got settled and said, "I'm ready," as she slammed her door.

He jerked his head and put the car in gear, knowing that the lane out was rather bumpy, and it was going to be a little bit until they were on a smooth road. Michigan had fierce winters and went through periods of freezing and thawing in both fall and spring, and it was difficult to keep the roads nice.

Thankfully the road to Blueberry Beach had recently been repaved, so he hoped to not encounter too many bumps, but he knew it was going to be a stressful ride for Gram.

"Keep me appraised if you feel like we need to call an ambulance because she's going into shock or something, I think it'll be okay if we meet them somewhere."

He really had no idea. In the city, he would call an ambulance, because the sirens would make it so that they could definitely get places faster, not to mention, parking at a hospital in town could be complicated. But the Blueberry Beach Hospital would be just as easy for him to reach, and since there were no volunteer EMTs anywhere closer, it just made sense.

But sometimes things that made sense weren't always the best choices, and sometimes he didn't know what he didn't know. That was always a danger.

Still, he made the best decision he could with the information that he had, and Birdie seemed like she agreed.

It was a long ride, and Gram moaned twice. Each time, it ripped at his insides and shot pain straight through him. He hated to think of the sweet lady who was always helping others suffering and in pain.

But there wasn't anything he could do except keep driving. He was already driving way faster than he should. But finally, the lights of Blueberry Beach came into view. It was just a little bit further until they got to the hospital.

He pulled up to the hospital emergency doors, the blue light overhead shining on the windshield, and he spotted a wheelchair in the foyer between the two double doors.

"I'm gonna run in and get that wheelchair, and then we can maybe put her in that?"

"Yeah. Good idea."

He could carry her in, but every step he took would bounce her leg. It would be better for her to ride in a wheelchair, even though he thought either way would be painful, since it would be hard to rest her leg against anything and not have it hurt.

The outside door opened, and he was able to grab the wheelchair from where it rested between the two.

There was a lady sitting at the desk, and she saw him. He lifted a hand and then pushed the wheelchair out.

He didn't know what the protocols were. Every hospital was probably different, and he wasn't exactly familiar with ERs. He'd gotten hurt a good bit playing hockey, but someone else had always been taking care of things. He hadn't had to make any decisions on his own about where he was going to get care. At times, he had to make decisions about how he was going to heal, but most decisions were made for him. And he had never really appreciated that until now.

Twenty-One

Birdie knew that a broken leg wasn't necessarily a death sentence. In fact, of all the things that could happen to Gram, this was probably one of the best, but she hated seeing her gram in pain. Plus, she knew complications were not out of the question. Both from the leg and from other injuries that her gram might not even realize she sustained.

She didn't want to borrow trouble though, and she really appreciated Wesley's calm, competent demeanor. He hadn't taken charge, but he'd guided her in a way that felt natural and right. Like they were working together, not against each other. And if she wanted something, he didn't argue.

She appreciated that. She thought he might be going to give her a hard time about wanting the blanket, but he'd gone with it.

Regardless, he'd driven there, faster than she ever would have, and was now helping get Gram in a wheelchair. Again, the blanket came in handy.

"It might be easier to take her out backward," Wesley said as he parked the wheelchair by the door.

"You might be right. The blanket might make it so that we could just pull her out. What do you think of that, Gram?"

"Yeah," Gram said. She wasn't quite as perky as she had been. And Birdie exchanged a look with Wesley. She wasn't sure whether it was shock, or whether her gram was just getting tired. Or maybe the pain was that bad.

There was no point asking about it. They were almost there.

Wesley hadn't said anything else, but he grabbed the handles of the wheelchair and steered it around the other side of the car. She ran around ahead of him and opened the door.

"All right. I'm going to pull on the blanket until I can't, and then maybe Birdie will pull on the blanket while I steady you and probably lift you the last few inches."

"All right," Gram said, her voice sounding a little bit stronger than it had the last time.

"It sounds like a plan to me," Birdie said, wanting to let him know she understood what he was saying. They were just going to do their best and try not to drop her, basically.

As scattered as it was, it was nice to think that they had a plan now.

He tugged on the blanket while she got her hands on it as well, one hand between his and one hand on her side to try to make sure she was pulling straight back and not tugging the blanket out from underneath.

They handed the blanket off flawlessly as he took one hand and put it behind her back and then another hand underneath her legs.

And just like he said, they were able to scoot her into the wheelchair with only a few inches where she was suspended over the ground.

He settled her down while Birdie adjusted her leg.

"Try not to mess with your other leg," she said. "Do you want me to close the footrest and put it to the side?" she asked, looking up into her gram's face, which was white and a little pasty looking.

A thrill of fear shot through her, but she closed her eyes, took a breath, and opened them again.

"No. We'll just go in like this."

"Hang in there, you're doing a great job," Wesley said, putting one hand on Gram's shoulder as he said it.

Gram nodded, and Wesley said, "You want to wheel her in so I can take the car and park it?"

"Oh. Sure. Good thinking," she said, tucking the blanket in so she wouldn't run over it and going behind the wheelchair, grabbing the handles.

Wesley unhooked the brakes that she hadn't even realized he'd set, and she appreciated again the fact that he was there. She wouldn't have thought to set the wheelchair's brakes, and it might have slid out from underneath them if she were trying to do it herself.

Although she might have called an ambulance, which would have made Gram's time to the hospital twice as long.

She pulled back and wheeled around to the spot at the sidewalk that had the ramp. Pushing, she said, "I didn't realize wheelchairs were this difficult. Everyone else makes them look so easy."

"Maybe you'll get used to it someday, but hopefully not with me. Not now anyway."

She felt like her gram was way too young to be in a wheelchair. She acted young. A person's seventies didn't exactly say spring chicken, but it was a lot younger than it used to be, and she expected to have her gram well into her nineties. In fact, they joked at times about celebrating her one hundredth birthday. She had every intention of her gram getting there.

She felt strangely alone as she pushed the wheelchair and the doors opened. It was odd how quickly she got used to Wesley being at her side. Helping her make decisions, just giving her confidence with his presence. He didn't even have to say anything.

But she forged ahead, blinking in the bright lights, pushing straight to the desk.

"Oh goodness, what happened?" the receptionist said, peering over the counter at Gram in the wheelchair.

Gram didn't answer right away, so Birdie spoke. "She fell down the steps of the porch, and she thinks her leg is broken. I didn't even think to check it, we just put her in the car and brought her here."

"All right. I'm going to need some information, but I've alerted them in the back, and someone will be out to get her while I get your information from you. Is that okay?"

"Yeah. I know she's in a lot of pain. We had to bump it some in order to get her in here."

"I understand. We will get that taken care of as soon as we can."

The receptionist had barely stopped speaking when a man came out of the double glass doors, dressed in scrubs with his head wrapped in a hairnet.

"Hey there. I hear we have a potential broken leg. Is it okay if I take you back?"

"Yes, and I'd like some pain medicine right now, please," Gram said.

Birdie tried not to roll her eyes. Gram would get things straightened out back there.

"What's your name, ma'am?" the man said as he held up the iPad that was strapped to his arm.

Gram said her name, the man typed a few things in, and then he pushed her back through the glass doors from which he'd come.

"All right. I'm going to need her insurance information, as well as her Social Security number if you have it. If not, I can fill this in later, but we'll get everything we can."

"All right," Birdie said as cool air hit the back of her neck and she turned.

Wesley strode in, looking so beloved and familiar she almost turned and ran, throwing her arms around him, like she was two instead of almost thirty.

She went around to where the lady indicated and sat down, pulling the information that she had known she was going to need from Gram's purse which she'd grabbed when she turned off the oven.

"If you'd like to go back with your grandma... It is your grandma?" the lady said, tilting her head and touching Birdie's hand across the counter that separated them.

"Yes. It's my gram, and—"

"Then he can stay here and give me the information that I need, and I'll allow you to go back with her if you want to."

"Really?" Birdie said, not even thinking that that would have been possible.

"Sure," the receptionist said, and then she added, "If you want to step back over here, I'll take you back, and if you give him the info, I'll be back to get it from him."

"Do you mind?" she asked Wesley as she stood, realizing that she hadn't even checked with him.

"Go be with your gram. I'm fine. I'll take care of it. Although, it would be weird rifling through her purse."

"Do whatever you need to do to find information you need. She told me that whatever you can't find, you can fill in later."

"All right. I'll be back if they'll let me. Otherwise, I'll be in the waiting room. Text me if you learn anything."

"I will. Thank you so much."

He didn't have to stay. He was no relation and had no skin in this game, but it didn't sound like he was going anywhere at all. In fact, he'd done nothing but help.

She had just never met anyone like him. Someone who was so willing to sacrifice whatever he needed to in order to be with her. Help her, even spend time with her.

She met the receptionist at the front desk and noticed for the first time that off to the left there were folks sitting in chairs in what must have been the open waiting area. There were about five folks in chairs and a TV in each corner. She couldn't really tell what was on, but four of the five folks were watching TV, and one was sitting in their chair, head to chest, and looked like they were sleeping. She assumed that's where she would go to find Wesley. If she needed to.

"You need a badge to get back through here," the lady said as she scanned her badge on the little box on the wall, and the door started to open.

"Only one person at a time. We don't let more than that back here, or it tends to get crowded." She looked around. "But on a night like tonight, we would probably make an exception. It's pretty slow."

"Oh. So maybe Wesley can come back when he's done?"

"Sure. I don't see any reason why not. If he wants to. Sometimes people don't like blood or pain or whatever, and they'd rather wait in the waiting room. As long as she has someone to sit and hold her hand. We found that that helps, not only pain levels, but anxiety as well. Although we have pills to handle that." The receptionist chattered as they walked back to the second door on the right, and she pointed. "There's your gram."

"Thank you," Birdie said as she walked slowly in the room. Gram still talked to the man who had taken her back. He had a stethoscope around his neck and was just hanging up the cuff on a blood pressure machine.

"It's a little low. We'll be keeping an eye on her for shock. Right now, I have a heated blanket on her, and I've ordered X-rays. They'll be coming to get her shortly."

"All right, wow. You guys don't mess around."

"Tonight, we're not that busy, but sometimes we are, and it's helpful to have things move along if we can. Although, sometimes when you rush, you make mistakes. There's a fine line." The man's brown eyes were friendly but serious, and he gave her a small smile before he walked out of the room.

"Are you okay, Gram?" she asked, even though she knew there really was a very limited number of things that she could do.

"I'm thirsty."

"All right. I'll tell the nurse whenever he gets back, unless you want me to go find him." She was trying to think of any reason why her gram couldn't have a drink. She might as well ask.

"I can wait. I just don't want to wait all night. If I have to wait until after I get the X-rays, that's fine. But I want a tall glass of water waiting for me when I get back. Preferably with a slice of lemon and ice as well."

"I'll see what I can do, Gram."

People would think Gram was a princess the way she was ordering her ice water, but it was just Gram's way of taking control of the situation, at least that's what Birdie figured. Maybe she was wrong. Maybe there was something else going on. Or maybe Gram really was desperate for a glass of ice water with a slice of lemon in it.

She shook her head at the thought. Her grandma was something else.

It wasn't long until the male nurse came to take her back for the X-rays. Birdie was not allowed to go.

"We'll bring her back as soon as she's done. If she's going to have to have any type of treatment, the doctor will talk to you here first."

"All right," she said, wondering what in the world they might mean by any type of treatment. That almost sounded like...they thought it might be more than a break? Or maybe that's just the way they talked.

She decided not to borrow trouble, although she had to admit she was relieved when Wesley walked in just a moment or two after her grandma left.

"You just missed her. They took her back for X-rays."

"Wow. That was fast."

"That's what I said. But the nurse said they try to do things speedily but not rushed. They don't like to make mistakes."

"Nobody does. But mistakes are a little bit more concerning in a place like this."

He walked in, and she thought he might pace, but there was a chair against the wall, and he sank down in it. Facing her in the seat that she had chosen beside where the bed had been before they wheeled the entire bed to the X-ray room, wherever that was.

"Are you holding up okay?" Wesley asked.

"Yeah. I mean, I keep telling myself it's just a broken leg, and I don't need to be so worked up. But... I'm worried. You know. She's my gram."

"I know. I don't want anything to happen to her. But God's got this. I've been praying. And I'm betting you have too."

"When I think about it. I've been more worried than peaceful though. So I probably haven't been praying enough."

"That's okay. This is just practice for the next time."

"That's not reassuring," she said. The idea that there would be a next time. Or a time after that.

"I don't want to be doom and gloom, but if you're going to get married and have children, you're probably going to spend some time in the ER. Maybe even for yourself. You just might as well reconcile yourself to the fact that you're going to trust God every time. I think it gets easier."

"You've been in the ER?"

"Not for myself, not for Gramps, but with my grandma. I got to the point where I hated hospitals, and I started to get a sick feeling every time we pulled in the parking lot. They smell bad, nobody's happy, and it's just basically a miserable environment. But it's more about my attitude. Right?"

"But you lost your gram."

He took a breath, blew it out, and said, "I know I don't need to correct you, so don't take it that way, but I don't think about it like that.

I think about it like God took her. Or she got a promotion. Or she's happier. But it's true she's not with us anymore, and...for a long time, that was hard. I did some things I wish I wouldn't have and didn't handle it as well as I could have. I guess maybe that's why I was telling you that you need to be prepared. It's what I wish someone would have told me. It's inevitable. Not that I want to be negative all the time, I just want to know that I can see these things and go through them with God's help, not scared, not upset, and not anxious. I want to trust God."

"You're really good at pep talks," she said, and he winced a little. Which was odd.

"Did I say something wrong?"

"No. I'm sorry. I guess I just wish I was a little better or had been a little better. Like I said, after Gram died, I didn't exactly go off the deep end, but I did do some things I wish I wouldn't have."

"I see. I suppose those are things you could tell me about?"

"Those are things I'll write in my book. Maybe. I haven't yet."

And that's when it hit her. Her eyes got big, and he must have seen that all of a sudden she had an epiphany, because he looked around and then said, "What?"

Twenty-Two

"All the things that Gram signed up for. Who is going to do those things now?"

Wesley stared at Birdie and then blinked. And then he shrugged his shoulders. "I guess they just won't get done."

"You don't know my gram very well. She's going to kill herself to do them."

"Then you and I'll take it over until she can."

"That's a lot of stuff!" She didn't even want to do it. And it was her gram! He couldn't possibly know what he was talking about.

"One person did it. Surely the two of us together can get it done. What else are we doing?" He grinned. "Besides hiding."

"That's not funny." It was too close to the truth. Probably for both of them, but for her in particular. Maybe he could joke about it, but she didn't want to be found out.

"We'll talk to her about it. She's not going to be laid up forever. After she gets the cast on, she might be able to get around, once the pain isn't so bad."

"I'll have to have someone watch her if I'm running around doing all of her things."

"What about Becky? She has us as customers in the evening, but it didn't sound like she was too busy any other time. Maybe she'd be happy to have something to do, and she was going to be a nurse."

"I want to worry about something, and you're making it impossible."

He laughed. "Is that my job?"

"If it is, you're doing it admirably. I probably should give you a raise."

"I'd take a raise."

He had her laughing again, and suddenly all the worry that she had had didn't exactly evaporate, but it didn't feel so heavy either. She felt like she could handle things. She felt like she had been reminded that God was beside her, and Wesley was there too. He sat in the chair, his ankle resting on his knee, looking relaxed and confident.

He wasn't filling the silence with idle chitchat, but he was being reasonable and rational and making her laugh. She couldn't think of anyone else she'd rather have.

"Oh. By the way, Gramps texted me back. I guess he got up to go to the bathroom and put his glasses on long enough to check his phone. Anyway, he knows where we are, and if you need anything handled, he's there."

"Thanks for letting me know," she said, sitting in the chair thinking about how grateful she was that this had happened when Wesley was around. And then, rather than thinking about what might have happened if he hadn't been there, she thought about how perfect God's timing was, that He allowed it to happen when she had help. When she had someone beside her. Even though she could have called multiple people or hired someone if she had to. It was just nice that she hadn't had to.

A noise in the hall had them turning their heads toward the door as the bed with Gram in it came through, then the nurse.

"All right. She did well. Got the pictures that we need, and after the doctor looks at them and possibly consults with some other people, he will be in to talk with you," the nurse said as he pushed Gram's hospital bed back in the room.

"My water?" she asked, not in a strident tone, but with enough confidence that Birdie was sure it would get someone running.

"I'll be back with it. I figured your family would like to see you first."

"I suppose you're right. They don't know that you didn't take me back there to murder me on the X-ray table."

Birdie smiled. She seemed like she was feeling a lot better. Her voice had its old spunk back to it, and she was ordering people around. Definitely her gram was back.

She exchanged a smile with Wesley. Everything had turned out so much better than she thought.

Her gram got settled, with her blankets tucked in, and the nurse came back with her water.

"Thank you," she said, giving him a kind look. Almost a queenly look. Birdie had to bite back another grin.

"My pleasure, ma'am. The doctor's going to be in here shortly." He walked out without saying anything more.

"Did they give you an idea of how they thought it was broken?" Birdie asked, knowing that she was assuming that the leg was broken, but she kind of felt like her gram had lived long enough that she ought to know.

"No, and I didn't get a good look at the pictures. Or I probably could have figured it out on my own."

"Mrs. Pollock?" the doctor said, walking in the room with an iPad in front of him. He scrolled up and then looked up over the top of it at Gram.

"I've heard you're quite a character," he said by way of greeting, holding his hand out. "I'm Dr. Studer."

"Good to meet you, doc," Gram said. "I'll have you know it's past my bedtime."

"All right. We'll try to get you taken care of and out of here as quickly as possible." He held his hand out to Birdie. "Dr. Studer."

"Nice to meet you, doctor. I really like the efficiency of this hospital. I feel like we barely have time to catch our breath before something else is happening. And that's not the complaint you usually hear in the emergency room."

"No, it's not," the doctor said, walking over and holding his hand out to Wesley, who had stood up, shaking his hand and looking him in the eye. "Wesley Moffat," he said, and the doctor nodded, squinting his eyes a bit. "Think I've heard of you. Or you have a name that's similar to somebody famous."

"I get that all the time," Wesley said without missing a beat. Birdie wanted to snort. But she didn't.

"All right, I've got some good news for you. The leg is fractured but not broken. You can see on this X-ray right here." He held the iPad up for Gram to look at. Birdie leaned over so she could see too. Wesley moved to the other side so all three of them were looking at it.

"See this little thing right here that looks like a hair. That's the crack in your bone. It could have been a lot worse, and often is in folks your age. I bet you're pretty active."

"I am, and I don't want this to change that, so get me better as fast as you can."

"We don't want to rush things and can't to some extent. If you want it to go faster, you're going to have to talk to the Lord about that."

That comment made Birdie like the man even more. The fact that he wasn't trying to say that something else was causing the healing but gave God the credit He deserved. It was probably a crazy thing, but it made her trust the doctor more.

"Now, something like this usually takes six to eight weeks to heal. That's in an average adult. You're a little bit older, but you have being active in your favor, and I see you have pretty good bones, just looking at these X-rays. The fact that the break wasn't any worse than what it was is likely due to that. Possibly, you'll be on the lower end of that time estimate, but again, we don't want to rush things. So, the good news is, you're not going to have to stay off your leg. Once the pain eases, you can get around all you want to. But the bad news is, we are definitely going to be casting your foot along with your lower leg." He grinned. "More good news is that we don't have to cast your knee. As long as the healing takes place the way it needs to. If it doesn't, we'll take more draconian measures."

"All right. Where do I go to get the cast?"

"That is something I wanted to talk to you about. We actually happen to have an orthopedic surgeon in the building tonight, and that's how I'm able to give you all of this information. Usually an ER doctor just tells you it's fractured and makes an appointment for the orthopedics, and puts the splint on and gets you some pain meds. We can cast it tonight if you want to. He said he'd come on down and do that."

"All right. Send him down."

"Well, you said it was past your bedtime, and you wanted to get home, so I don't want to hold you up. I can sign off on these orders and you can be out of here in fifteen minutes. Or if you decide to get it casted, it's probably going to be another hour or two."

"Let's cast it tonight," her gram said, surprising no one.

"All right. I'll go out and talk to Dr. Lemen, and he'll be in with his staff. You'll talk to him, and then one of his staff will put the actual cast on."

"Interesting," Gram said, although Birdie didn't think she cared. She just wanted to get it taken care of. And Birdie couldn't blame her.

The doctor left, and Gram looked steadily at Birdie. "He said I'd be able to get around as soon as I can handle the pain. So I wouldn't need you for any more than a week. Do you think you could handle everything I signed up for?"

Birdie had to laugh at herself. Gram had barely even allowed the doctor to get out of the room before she was trying to take care of all of the things that she did.

If she was going to do what she wanted to do, she would say no. She didn't want to take over all of Gram's responsibilities. She hadn't signed up for them, and she'd cautioned Gram not to sign up for them either.

"I don't want to let anyone down, and I just spent all that time talking to the pastor."

Birdie knew the pastor would understand. After all, Gram had a broken leg! But she also knew how important those things were to Gram. And even more than that, she knew that Gram would do it for her.

But first and foremost, she should do things for people, regardless of how they treated her. Still Gram had been so good for her, she could hardly not do anything Gram asked and even things she didn't.

"I'll do whatever I need to, for as long as I need to, to keep your obligations met. You know I would never let you down. Not if I can help it." That was the truth.

"And I'll give her a hand. We already talked about it, and Birdie knew that you were going to need some help. I know she was happy to do it for you."

Gram snorted. "Probably not, especially since she tried to talk me into not signing up for so much. And now, I have to admit that she was right. Which is great, but I appreciate you guys making sure that not only am I taken care of here, but the things that are important to me are taken care of."

"Our pleasure," Wesley said easily.

"What famous person do you have the same name as?" Gram asked in an abrupt subject change, narrowing her eyes at Wesley.

"Somebody by the name of Wesley," Wesley said, shrugging his shoulders and grinning.

Birdie coughed out a laugh. "You asked for that one, Gram."

"It's the pain meds they gave me. They're making me a little loopy."

"I think you're naturally a little loopy. And *did* they give you pain meds?"

"I don't think so. I just pretended to myself they did. I keep thinking that my leg should feel better any time."

She grinned again, grateful that not only was her gram okay, but that her sense of humor was back and she sounded almost like herself.

"Excuse me," a voice said from the side of the room, and Birdie moved over. "I need to give Mrs. Pollock her pain meds." A girl, wearing scrubs and looking young, came in holding a pack of pills in her hand.

"All right. You already have your water. Do you think you can swallow these?" she asked, holding up the little packet of meds.

"If it's gonna help me with my pain, I can swallow anything," Gram said.

Birdie moved back and stood beside Wesley. "Thank you. I do really appreciate everything you've done."

"Sounds to me like our jobs are just starting."

The aide had not left the room before a man wearing a white coat came in.

He introduced himself as Dr. Lemen and was a little more businesslike than the first doctor.

He explained what was going on and asked again if it was okay with Gram to have a cast put on her leg.

She had to sign some release forms, and while she was doing that, several techs came in with the supplies necessary to do the cast.

"It's a little crowded in here. I'm gonna go out and pull the car around, and hang out in the waiting room. If that's okay with you," Wesley said as they shuffled around trying to get things organized in the small room.

"Sure. That's fine. I think I'll stay in here, just in case Gram needs me, but it looks to me like they're not going to be taking a long time for anything."

"I wish all hospital emergency rooms were like this. I know Blueberry Beach is probably a less populated area, and this is a great hospital, but it's very nice."

"I agree," she said as he walked out.

She didn't want him to go, feeling like she was losing some of her support.

But the Lord was still there, and she wasn't going to worry. Still, she felt a little wobbly as she faced the room without Wesley. Funny how it didn't take long at all for her to get used to having him by her side.

Twenty-Three

Wesley walked in the hospital, leaving the car parked just outside. The lot was pretty much deserted, and he parked slightly back, on the off chance that someone might pull in and need to rush in. That way, his car would be out of the way, but not so far Gram couldn't make it there.

He couldn't get back through the glass doors without a badge, so he stood at the edge of the waiting room. There was no door on it; it was just a large open area where chairs had been set up and a TV played in both corners. Someone had turned the TV up since the last time he had walked through, although he wasn't sure which of the four people who were still sitting there might have been the culprit. They all had their eyes glued on them, three on the one in the far corner, and one on the opposite set.

They must have been playing different things, but Wesley didn't pay much attention. He was more interested in getting to Birdie, and he considered asking the receptionist to let him back.

But since he expected her back anytime, and since the little room was already really crowded, he didn't.

It turned out that he only waited about ten minutes before he saw them coming down the hall.

He went and stood by the glass doors that opened automatically as they stepped near.

"I wondered where you went."

"I couldn't get back in without a badge, and I expected you guys would be done soon. I have the car right here out front," he said.

Gram was in a wheelchair with her foot cast and her face no longer pinched in pain.

"We had to sign our life away, but beyond that, we should be good."

"Perfect." They turned to go.

For the first time that evening, they saw someone else coming in, and so they moved over, giving them plenty of room to pass.

In the short amount of time that they stood there, there was a commercial playing on TV, and for some reason, it caught his attention.

Looking over, he saw a clean-shaven guy, running a finger over his face and holding up a razor, talking about what a great razor it was.

There weren't a whole lot of times in his life where he wanted to sink through the floor, but that was one of them.

The dude on the screen was him.

He could see the fine print at the bottom of the screen that said *Wesley Moffat. Actual player for the Icebreaker hockey team.*

Hopefully it was too small for anyone else to read, and the only reason he could read it was because he knew what it said.

But he heard a little gasp beside him, and he turned his head slowly, first looking at Gram who watched the people coming in. Someone was bleeding, and they were holding their right arm, while someone else held a bloodied bandage to their head.

As his eyes continued to move, and his head followed them, Birdie came into view. Her eyes were glued on the screen.

"All right then, let's go, before someone else comes in here and starts bleeding all over the place," he said mostly just to say something, not because he was all of a sudden in a big rush to get out. Even though Gram was surely ready to go home.

When was Birdie going to say something? Had she seen his name? Had she recognized him? Or had she just thought the guy was familiar?

A full beard was always uncomfortable for him, although many of his teammates grew them in the winter. But he often had scruff on his face. A few days' worth of growth on his face. And he'd made sure it stayed there since he'd come to Raspberry Ridge, hoping not to be recognized.

Would she be able to recognize him despite that?

The commercial was more than a year and a half old, and he matured some since then, although he figured he probably looked the same. Or almost. Just a year and half's worth of age on his face, but at his age, it didn't make a big difference.

Either she did or she didn't. He couldn't do anything about it now and wasn't going to talk to her about it in front of Gram.

"The front seat has more legroom. Do you think we'd better put her there?" he asked as Birdie walked silently beside him as they stepped out into the cool night and turned right to go to their car.

"That's a good idea," she said as she walked ahead, opening the front door.

"I think I can get myself on my feet, I just might need someone to help me down."

"How about you hold on to my forearms, and Birdie will make sure you don't hit your head on the car."

"That sounds easy enough," Gram said.

"Whatever those meds are, we need to get a lifetime subscription. They make her agreeable."

"Oh, you hush." Gram gave him a light slap on the forearm before she grabbed it.

He laughed, figuring that she didn't mind his teasing at all. She probably appreciated laughing.

Birdie was strangely quiet. It was only a matter of time until Gram noticed.

Maybe she was trying to figure out what the lines had said, or maybe she was trying to figure out what she knew about him. He'd been in the news. Although, someone who didn't follow sports might not have heard anything.

"All right, I'll take the wheelchair back," he said as they got her gram in, and he pushed the door closed.

She didn't say anything but opened the door and got in the back.

He wasn't going to worry about it. He reminded himself of that as he was walking around the car. He didn't think it would make a difference. She knew him. She'd been around him. She saw him. Shouldn't make a difference. He wouldn't have chosen for her to find out that way, but he couldn't undo it.

Still, the car was quiet as he maneuvered through the hospital parking lot and got out on the highway.

"Birdie, hand me my purse, please. I want to check and make sure that I put my phone in it. I think I did."

"Sure, Gram," Birdie said, scooting over a little and holding her purse out.

Gram took it, and Birdie continued to sit in the back. He was tempted to look in the rearview mirror, where he could see her easily now, but he didn't.

As he made the turn to get out on the interstate, he happened to look up at a billboard.

It was to the left, on the other side of the road. It was huge, and it showed full-body shots of a singer in skintight leggings and a dress that hit right above her knees. She had a microphone in her hand, and her mouth was open, like she was in the middle of singing a song.

Polly, the billboard read, *new album out this fall. Preorder now!*

He stared at the billboard, something making his eyes unable to turn away, and then, as clear as a bell, he knew exactly what it was.

Pollock was Birdie's last name. Polly was her gram's name. She had gotten her stage name either from her gram or from her last name. Birdie Pollock was Polly, pop superstar and international sensation. Quite possibly the most famous person on the planet.

Twenty-Four

Birdie sat on her bed, her phone in her hand.

She could hear her grandma's gentle snores, almost certainly aided by the pain meds she'd taken earlier.

Wes had left almost as soon as he'd helped get her in the house. Wesley Moffat, hockey superstar and currently suspended for the first four weeks of the season due to an off-ice brawl he'd incited at the end of the previous season.

She flipped the phone back and forth in her hand. She'd been searching on the internet since her grandma had fallen asleep. Reading every article she could get her eyes on, and they all said basically the same thing. Wes snapped at the end of the season. He'd been involved in several unnecessarily rough scuffles, even for hockey, on the ice, and the last brawl, outside a downtown Richmond pub, had sent two people to the hospital.

He had been the one who had instigated it all.

Because of his previous behavior, his penalty had been huge, and the Icebreakers had talked about trading him.

No trade had been made, and he was still set to start the season suspended until October.

She tried to reconcile the person she read about online to the person that she knew and had been hanging out with for the last two weeks. Kind and funny, gentle and sweet, he'd just helped her grandmother in and out of the emergency room, for goodness' sake.

He lived with his gramps. He ate supper at their house every night. He went to church. He was going to help her cover her gram's obligations.

She couldn't think of a bad thing to say about him.

But all of the stuff online looked terrible.

She just couldn't square the two things, and she hated that.

She was going to have to talk to him, particularly because she saw him looking at the billboard. She hadn't realized it was there. She hadn't seen it on the drive there, anyway.

One of those billboards that was lit up on both sides.

Regardless, she was going to have to think up what she was going to tell him about her… Or maybe not.

She fingered the other list that she had in her hand, the paper list that she had made out.

It listed all of her obligations for the week.

They were unending. Times and dates and what she had planned. Taken directly from Gram's planner. Birdie had copied it herself. Under Gram's supervision of course.

She balked at taking meals to shut-ins. She couldn't cook.

But her grandmother assured her that she would sit there and tell her what to do. Give her instructions on anything. And when she balked again, Gram said it was fine, her leg didn't hurt that much anyway, and she could stay on it long enough to cook a meal.

Of course, at that point, Birdie had said that she would do it, because what choice did she have?

Are you still up?

She looked at her phone as the text came in.

Wesley.

She stared at the text. Smiling despite herself. She didn't want to talk to him. Didn't want to have that conversation, didn't want the fairy tale to end.

Yes.

It's nice outside. Take a walk?

He wanted to take a walk? It was one o'clock in the morning.

She liked that, though. She liked that he didn't want to wait until morning, he wanted to see her now. Although, maybe it was because he wanted to tell her that he couldn't have anything to do with her anymore. Or maybe he decided she was worth a lot of money, and he wanted to put that ring on her finger right now.

She tried to scold herself for her negativity, but she remembered that he had said that she deserved to be a little bit cautious, because of the way she'd been hurt in the past. The people who had used her. The way people had latched onto her because of her fame and money and benefited from that, shamelessly.

Still, Wesley wasn't like that. She was sure.

She remembered what he had said about going to the Bible for the answers, about marrying another Christian.

For too long, she'd left her Christian roots behind while she'd sought fame and fortune.

Was that how God felt about her? That she'd left Him, not caring about what He said, while she benefited in every way possible.

She didn't want to think about the way she treated the Lord. Except, she needed to apologize, repent. Pastor Garnet talked about repentance in the sermon not long ago, and his message had resonated with her. Turning from her wickedness, turning from her sin. Even realizing what the person was doing was sin and going back to the Lord. She didn't even always notice that.

It had been a good sermon all around, and between that and Wesley's comment the other day—did she have to do what she was doing? Was there a way she could do less or not do it at all? The idea of giving up her career would be unthinkable to the majority of Americans, but just because it was unthinkable to some didn't mean it wasn't the right thing for her.

Her phone buzzed again with a reminder that she hadn't answered his text.

Okay.

She would go. She would talk. She would put her hand in God's hand and trust that He knew best.

She stood up, shoving her phone in her pocket, and her gram's snoring stopped.

"Birdie?" she asked.

"I'm right here, Gram. I was going outside for a little bit."

"I heard the neighbor's door slam closed. He must only care about the screen door to our house. He's a good man."

Her grandma turned her head, and before she started snoring again, Birdie said, "I'm going to go out to walk with him."

"He'll marry you. I'd do it if I were you."

Gram never said that to her before about any of the men she'd been with. Not that they were good, and not that she should marry them.

"I don't know if he'll have me, Gram. There is a lot that comes with me."

"You're worth it," Gram said softly.

"Go on back to sleep. I won't be long."

"I trust you with him," Gram said easily, and then it wasn't two breaths later she was snoring again.

Birdie smiled. Maybe that was the sign that she needed. Wesley had said that God didn't just speak through the Bible but also through trusted advisors.

Maybe that was God's trusted advisor.

She wasn't sure, but she had a good feeling. A feeling like this was the right thing. A feeling she'd never had before with anyone else.

She opened the door and did not allow the screen to slap as she exited, smiling at her gram waking up over the neighbor's screen door slamming.

That was such a gram thing to do.

"I almost thought you weren't coming."

"I sent a text," she said as she stepped off the porch. He was standing right at the bottom of the stairs, right where they had found Gram just hours earlier. She stopped at the bottom.

"You figured out who I was."

"I did."

"And?"

What did she say? She wasn't sure. How did she tell him that she didn't exactly understand, but she didn't hold it against him? Was that what she said?

"I think I love you." There. That wasn't expected, but it was true.

There was dead silence, and then he grunted and took a step forward, wrapping her in his arms and putting his head down next to hers, his lips by her ear, as he held her tight.

She wrapped her arms around him and held just as tight.

"I love you, too. I wasn't expecting to. I...didn't come here for this."

"Sometimes God works in ways we don't understand. And definitely in ways we don't expect."

"Polly? Am I right?"

"Yeah." She waited. What was he going to say?

"The internet has a lot to say about you."

She laughed. "It has a lot to say about you too."

"What do you say about you?" he asked.

That was a new question. What did she say about herself?

"I'm thinking about quitting. You put the idea into my head and... It's almost unheard of for a singer to walk away at the height of their career, but I'm seriously thinking about it."

"There was some country superstar that did that before, didn't they? Walked away when they were the most famous? Because of their family."

"Maybe, but I don't even have a family, it's just because...I want one."

"I sure hope you're thinking you want one with me. Because that's what I'm thinking."

"Yeah. Did you bring the ring?"

"Are you asking me to marry you?"

"I don't know. This is new territory for me. I guess I feel comfortable with that. But I can't get out of the tour that starts in January and goes through next June. I just can't. Too much money has been spent, too many people are on the hook for it. I can't cancel."

"Then don't."

"But you have hockey. You'll be playing games starting in October."

"I was thinking about retiring after the season. I don't need the money, I've been playing for the fun of it, but it's not even like that anymore. Plus, Gramps needs me." He paused. "Plus, I have a relationship I want to work on, and playing hockey doesn't give me a whole lot of time for relationships."

"So if we can make it until June, then...?"

"No. I don't want to wait until June. Not unless you demand it."

"I'm not gonna demand anything. I think there's two of us, and I think we should talk it out. It should not be me telling you what's going on."

"All right then, if you're going to ask me to marry you, I'm gonna say yes, and I'm gonna suggest we get married right away. And we'll make it work. Somehow."

"How? I don't understand?"

"We just make it. We're not going to allow things to come between us. We're not going to get upset over stupid stuff. We're going to spend as much time together as we can. I can't get out of hockey, you can't get out of performing, and I assume, the things that you were writing were songs?"

"Yeah. For my new album."

"Can you have albums without touring?"

"Sure. But you'll not make nearly as much money, and you gain more fans through touring."

"Could you just write songs and put out albums?"

"Yeah. That's kind of what I've been thinking. Other than maybe just giving it up completely. I don't want to have my attention pulled off my family. I don't want to lose my family because something else was more important."

"Me, either. Are you sure you want to take a chance on me? I did some pretty questionable things after my grandma died."

"I think you can be excused for your grief, but I'll say after knowing you, you're taking steps to figure out what went wrong, make sure that it doesn't happen again. Weren't you the one who was telling me that we needed to be prepared for these things?"

He laughed. "Are you throwing my words up in my face?"

"It's a bad habit I have. Does that bother you?"

"I love you, whether you have bad habits or not. Or maybe, your bad habits make you human, and I love that about you."

"It's funny, so many people look at Polly and think that she is perfect. That there couldn't be anything wrong with her. I appreciate knowing that you're cognizant that I'm going to screw up. Lots probably."

"I think you can expect the same from me, but hopefully not on the scale that I did last spring."

"I can't imagine how hard that must have been. To lose your gram, who was like a mother to you, and have to continue to play, dealing with your gramps, seeing his grief."

"That was probably the hardest thing. Seeing him grieve, not knowing how to help him." He pulled back a little, and she looked up into his face. "I'd like to kiss you. Is that okay?"

She smiled and nodded. "Maybe I should ask you to marry me first?"

"Hurry up."

She laughed. "I'm only going to do this once. I better get it right."

"All right. I've been waiting all evening for this. I suppose I can wait a few more minutes while the woman ponders a sentence that should be very easy—will you marry me?"

"I'm an artist, I'm a creative, I put words together for a living. It has to be just perfect."

"All right. I want to kiss you first, and then you can ask me later." He started to lower his head. She realized he was absolutely serious.

And then she realized, she was perfectly okay with that.

Epilogue

"This is our last ride for a while," Birdie said as Becky held the reins of her horse while she mounted.

"I heard you two were leaving for a bit," Becky said, knowing that she'd also heard that they were a true couple as well. They were perfect for each other. She could see that right from the start. They reminded her of the way Rodney and she had felt so right.

The thought sent a pang through her which she tried to ignore. The reason she'd come to Raspberry Ridge was to start a new life without him. It had been too painful in Strawberry Sands, even though she had an adopted family who loved her and a job she looked forward to going to each and every day.

Sometimes a person just had to get away.

"We'll be back," Wes said, with a tender look at Birdie. So sweet and with such longing in it that Becky could hardly stand it. Why couldn't that be her?

But no, she was not going to question God's direction for her life, she reminded herself as Birdie and Wes rode away, their hands linked between them, their horses' tails flowing softly in the lake breeze. And that's what she loved - the lake and the horses and the freedom to work doing what she loved all day. Sure, money was tight and sure, sometimes she still thought about Rodney, but Raspberry Ridge was a great town, and she'd enjoyed getting to know everyone and finding where she fit into small town life.

After the two horses and riders disappeared down the beach, she walked to her mailbox, and grabbed the one letter that had been delivered earlier. A letter from home.

She smiled, tearing it open. One slip of paper fell out and she pulled out an unopened, postaged-marked letter.

Seeing the familiar handwriting of her adopted mom, she read the note first.

Dear Becky,

This note came for you yesterday and I considered not forwarding it on, but I decided that you were old enough to make your own choices. I'll write more over the weekend when I have more time, but I wanted to send this immediately.

Love,
Mom

Becky appreciated her mother so much. Especially since she could tell immediately that the handwriting on the unopened letter was Rodney's.

With trembling fingers, she opened it, took a breath and said a short prayer before reading.

Dearest BecPet,

She swallowed hard at his use of the nickname he'd given her so many years ago.

I can't find you on social media and when I was home earlier this summer, your parents said you'd requested that they not tell me where you went.

I know I deserve this and so much more, but I promise I can explain everything. It wasn't what you thought it was. But, more than that, I want what we'd always talked about - you and me. The women I've met at school and in my job aren't anywhere near what you are. They can't compare. You're truly one of a kind. I knew that the first night you crawled into my bedroom, looking for food, and nothing more.

Those were the days, weren't they?

I hate the idea that I've become what my dad is - I haven't, and I really would like to be able to talk to you. It's killing me that you might think I broke my word.

Please reply to the address on the envelope. At least allow me to explain. Even if there isn't an opportunity for us to be together, we can still be friends, right?

Please respond.

Yours,
Rodney

Becky fingered the paper, trying to keep the tears in her eyes from falling down her cheeks.

Rodney had come to her high school graduation. They'd been on the front porch when everyone else had gone in for the night and she thought he was going to kiss her. He'd touched her cheek with his fingers, so gentle and sweet, and he'd whispered that he wanted to.

She'd told him that she'd been waiting for him forever. Maybe it was the wrong thing to say because he'd pulled away and hurried off without explanation. Every time she'd seen him after that he'd been distant, until she'd gone on a surprise visit to see him the past spring.

What a mistake.

She'd surprised him and some woman in a very loving embrace. She hadn't meant for him to see her, but she supposed she'd made a noise that had drawn his attention, but she'd managed to get away, even though he called after her.

That was when she'd moved to Raspberry Ridge and deleted all her social media accounts.

The breeze caused the paper in her fingers to rattle and she looked back down, having forgotten she was even holding it.

Should she allow him to explain? And what if he did? Did it matter? He could see whomever he wanted to. There was no rule that said he had to wait for her. Plus, she was more than old enough now, if that had been his problem when she was only eighteen.

She wasn't sure.

Tomorrow she'd be going to sit with Gram, and Gram always seemed to have a lot of wisdom. Maybe between her and her adopted mother, Becky could figure out whether to listen to her head, which told her that Rodney was a cheater just like his dad, or her heart, which told her that he was a good man and he hadn't broken any spoken vows. He'd just broken her trust, because she'd always believed they were meant to be together.

So much so that she'd never even looked at anyone else. Maybe she should.

It wasn't too late.

Taking a breath, still unsure what she was going to do, she turned and walked slowly back to the barn.

Join Jessie's list and be the first to know about new releases and sales on her books!

Order Beside the Rolling Waves, the next book in the Raspberry Ridge series where Becky is reunited with Rodney and they work to move past the secrets that are keeping them apart and build a life together in Raspberry Ridge.

Sneak peek of Beyond the
Setting Sun

Becky Peck opened a bleary eye and lifted one tentative hand out of the warm cocoon of her covers, slapping around on her almost freezing nightstand, trying to find her phone to shut off the alarm.

Finally, her groping fingers hit the snooze button, and she yanked her hand from the chilly air back underneath her cozy blankets. She had at least seven on her bed. And she wore a set of long underwear, two T-shirts, a long-sleeve T-shirt, a sweatshirt, and a puffer vest on the top, plus three or four layers on the bottom, along with a thin pair of socks underneath two warm wool pairs.

Her toes were still cold.

That probably meant her blankets had shifted during the night, but instead of trying to fix the blankets, she just pulled herself into a ball and used one of her hands to try to warm up her toes while closing her eyes and enjoying a couple more minutes of blessed rest.

Her day was going to be busy from the time her feet hit the floor until she fell into bed tonight. And she really should get out of bed and get it started.

But she dreaded the cold.

Her small apartment above the horse stable where she kept her precious babies was heated, but she kept the heat down to the very lowest it would go, just warm enough to keep the water lines from freezing. She couldn't afford the heat bill, not with the feed bill she had, plus the rent for the stable, and she did try to buy food for herself with whatever was left.

She ought to have health insurance, but she couldn't even think about that.

She wiggled around, trying to get the toes on her other foot where she could reach them. She moved so much, she knew she wasn't going back to sleep. So she might as well get up.

Bracing herself for the cold, dreading it, and wishing, just once, she could turn the heat up as high as she wanted, she took a deep breath and then threw the covers off, throwing her feet out of bed and going quickly to the bathroom.

It didn't take long at all to get dressed in her work clothes and pour a steaming hot cup of coffee.

She didn't really like coffee, and she had never needed it to wake up, but the warmth was what she craved, and she'd gotten herself hooked on the caffeine in the process. Not that it mattered.

Sometimes she wondered if anything mattered.

She'd always wanted to be around horses, it was her dream, but...she was sinking further and further into debt, and she had absolutely nothing to show for it.

Last summer, she hadn't made enough money on the carriage rides she gave tourists to even pay for the feed bill, let alone the farrier and vet bills, and the idea that she might eventually need another horse could cause her heart to stop for a couple of seconds. It certainly wasn't enough to support her. She did that by cleaning houses. But she only had so much time that she wasn't taking care of her horses, especially in the winter when ice needed to be broken, water hauled, snow scraped, and horses manually exercised, because she didn't want to chance them slipping on ice in the pasture. They were too expensive, too valuable, and she loved them too much for that. A horse with a broken leg would have to be put down.

She wrapped her hands around her coffee mug, eyeing her gloves by the door. She already had her coat on and her boots as well. The last thing to do was put her gloves on, pull her hat down over her ears, and head outside into the Michigan winter.

At least she didn't have to walk far to get to work, she thought to herself, not for the first time. She lived above the horse stable where her horses were stalled, so it smelled interesting in her apartment, but that didn't bother her, and her commute to work was her favorite part of her job.

No. Her favorite part of her job was the horses.

Draining the last of her coffee, she set the mug down on the counter to deal with later, grabbed her gloves, stuck them on, and then walked out the door.

Immediately the scent of horses and fresh manure hit her, and she breathed deeply. It smelled like home to her. Like safety and happiness and all the good things. That's part of the reason why she did what she did. Because she loved it. She loved this. Stepping out into a new day, breathing deeply of the smells that made her heart soar, and knowing that she got to do what so many people just dreamed of.

Sure, she lived below the poverty level, at a level that most people could not even begin to think of surviving at, and common luxuries, like toilet paper, were closely rationed, but...she loved her life.

There was only one thing missing.

"Good morning, Jasper," she said, walking down the stairs and petting the nose that stuck out of the stall.

Jasper was always up and waiting on her in the morning.

Sometimes Jethro, and the two mares, Velvet and Clementine, slept in a bit, but Jasper faced the day eagerly. He was always the one who wanted out, wanted to run, wanted to enjoy each new day, like it was a gift. He reminded her what a gift life really was. Sometimes she needed that reminder more than others.

"I wish I was as unaffected by the cold as you are," she said to Jasper as she scratched his wide forehead. Clydesdales were tall, a heavy draft breed. They were also extremely expensive, and that was part of what made her bills so high. She'd overextended herself buying all four of them.

She couldn't ask her adoptive parents, who would have insisted on giving her money and not allowed her to pay them back. Matt and

Jubilee Landry from Strawberry Sands had loaned her the money, and she knew that if she went to them and said she couldn't pay them back, they would be perfectly fine with it. They could afford to lose the money anyway. But there was something inside of her that absolutely would not allow her to not do what she said she was going to do. And when she asked to borrow the money, she told him she would pay a certain amount every month until it was paid back with interest.

It wasn't right to not keep her word. Because a man was only as good as his word. That went for women too.

She thought about someone who had not kept his word to her, and her heart broke a little, as it did every time she thought about Rodney.

But life went on, and she hadn't heard from him for a long time. And she wasn't going to worry about it. She was going to move on with her life.

She pushed her shoulders back and finished petting Jasper's wide forehead before she grabbed the bucket out of the gelding's stall, and another one out of Jethro's stall, and took them to the water hydrant at the front of the barn.

Hopefully it wasn't frozen this morning.

She saw the heat tape glowing and took that as a good sign.

Hooking the handle of the bucket over the back of the hydrant, she carefully turned it on so it didn't blast with full force at the bottom of the bucket, soaking her face and coat. She'd done that plenty of times and had done the rest of the morning chores with a frozen coat and frozen body. Getting her face flushed with cold water first thing on a subzero-temperature day served to wake a person up, that was for sure. But it also was exceptionally uncomfortable.

As the water filled the bucket, she grabbed her phone out.

Good morning, beautiful.

She smiled. It was Rick, her almost boyfriend.

She didn't take her gloves off to message him back, just used her nose to pull up the emojis and sent him a smiley face.

Rick would know she was working and understand.

Shoving her phone back in her pocket, she shut the water off, switched the buckets, and carefully turned the water back on. Then, while the second bucket was filling, she carried Jasper's bucket to him and opened the stall door, setting it down so he could drink his fill.

She'd go and fill it back up, and that time, she'd hook it into his stall.

The heat from the horse usually kept the water from freezing, but not always. It depended on the wind coming off of Lake Michigan and how low the temperatures dropped.

Grabbing a bucket from Velvet's stall, she hurried back, knowing from doing it over and over again that if she hurried, she could get there just as the bucket got full.

She timed it perfectly, shut the water off, hooked Velvet's bucket onto the water spout, turned it on, and hurried back to Jethro's stall.

It took a good fifteen minutes to completely water the horses, and then it was time to feed them.

Once they were fed, she would muck out their stalls, and then she would work on taking them out and giving them some exercise.

It wasn't strictly necessary, but she wanted them to be in good shape if she got a request for a carriage ride. Which, now that Christmas was over, bookings had slowed down to a trickle. Or maybe it had stopped altogether. She scrunched her nose up and tried to remember the last time she had a booking.

Last week? Two weeks ago?

She wasn't even sure what day it was. Sometime toward the end of February.

"Oh my darling, oh my darling, oh my darling Clementine. You were lost and gone forever, oh my darling Clementine." She sang to her horse as she scooped poop out of the stall, dumping it into the wheelbarrow that waited in the aisle.

Her phone buzzed again, and she tried to figure out who in the world that could be.

Rick had said good morning to her, but he knew that she would be working, and he wouldn't bother her unless there was a problem.

Was there a problem?

She stopped, leaned the manure fork against the wheelbarrow, and pulled her phone back out of her pants pocket.

There were two texts. Both from her sister, Rita. That was even more strange. Rita knew she didn't have a data plan. She paid for data as she used it with her TracFone. They didn't talk to each other unless it was strictly necessary.

Rick wasn't quite so considerate, and she gave him a little bit of grace, because she figured that when a man liked a woman, he wanted to talk to that girl.

She really wasn't sure how much Rick liked her, and they'd never said anything about being exclusive. Their relationship was one of those ones where she was kind of in limbo all the time, but it suited her just fine, because it wasn't like she was financially stable and ready for a serious boyfriend anyway.

He was. At least he should be. He had a good job, and he was at the point where he could support a wife and family.

She wasn't quite sure he could support a wife with four Clydesdales and a family, but she kinda hoped he was.

A little slice of unease sat on that thought for a moment before she pushed it aside. So life wasn't turning out quite the way she wanted it to. Or the way she thought it was going to. Or the way she had hoped. She had to move on. She couldn't wait around forever for someone who wasn't going to keep his word and who'd ghosted her years ago.

Opening up Rita's text with her nose, she blinked as she read the text, then read it again to be sure.

I need to talk to you.

The next text was just as mysterious.

Please. As soon as you can.

That was really weird.

She pulled a glove off with her teeth and held it in her mouth. Should she finish doing the horses? Was this like an emergency where... what? Her sister lived in a suburb of Chicago, and considering their upbringing, she'd done pretty well for herself. She had an apartment and a job, and while she had just broken up with her boyfriend of six months, a six-month relationship wasn't a terrible thing. Considering that Rita hadn't been raised in the best of conditions, it was pretty good that she was as stable as what she was.

She was more stable than Becky anyway.

But Becky had always had more pluck. More grit and determination. There weren't a whole lot of people who could live the way she was living and even enjoy it and be happy about it.

At least that's what she told herself anyway. Still, she decided that this was probably something that she ought to address immediately.

Knowing that she would get cold if she stopped working, she went into the small office, where she allowed herself the luxury of a space heater. She turned it on, pulled her other glove off, and sat on the folding chair in front of the heater so as not to waste any of the glorious warmth coming from it.

She wouldn't have it on for long, just long enough that her fingers wouldn't freeze as she pulled her sister's contact up and put her phone on speaker so she could put her gloves back on and turn the heater off.

"Becky. You didn't have to call me that fast."

"I sure did. You asked me to call you as soon as I could. You know that there isn't too much that I would have been doing that I wouldn't have dropped in order to talk to you right away. What's going on?"

"I got my test results back."

Sign up for Jessie's newsletter! Get a free book, access to exclusive bonus content, get fun and funny updates on her life on the farm and more!

A Gift from Jessie

View this code through your smart phone camera to be taken to a page where you can download a FREE ebook when you sign up to get updates from Jessie Gussman! Find out why people say, "Jessie's is the only newsletter I open and read" and "You make my day brighter. Love, love, love reading your newsletters. I don't know where you find time to write books. You are so busy living life. A true blessing." and "I know from now on that I can't be drinking my morning coffee while reading your newsletter – I laughed so hard I sprayed it out all over the table!"

Claim your free book from Jessie!

www.ingramcontent.com/pod-product-compliance
Lightning Source LLC
Chambersburg PA
CBHW031046310726
48969CB00007B/2141